THE MAGICAL BOOKSHOP: 5

Black BOOKS

LIZ HEDGECOCK

WHITE RHINO BOOKS

Copyright © Liz Hedgecock, 2021

All rights reserved. Apart from any use permitted under UK copyright law, no part of this publication may be reproduced, stored in a retrieval system, or transmitted, in any form or by any means, electronic, mechanical, photocopying, recording or otherwise, without the prior written permission of the copyright owner.

This is a work of fiction. Names, characters, businesses, places, events and incidents are either the products of the author's imagination or used in a fictitious manner. Any resemblance to actual persons, living or dead, or actual events is purely coincidental.

ISBN-13: 979-8788840451

*For Carol,
fellow author, reader, and friend*

Chapter 1

'Do we really need all this?' said Luke, as they walked down Charing Cross Road together, each carrying a loaded bag. 'Raphael said it was a Grade Four knowledge emergency.'

Jemma didn't answer him for a few moments, as she was concentrating on avoiding the icy patches on the pavement. It was late January, but winter showed no sign of retreating. Even at mid-morning, frost and occasional slush remained. 'I'd rather have too much gear than not enough,' she replied, eventually. 'Besides, you're with me, and it's your first time.'

Luke didn't respond, and they walked in silence until Jemma spied Charing Cross Library. 'Here we are,' she said, and unslung her knowledge emergency kitbag.

She had been to the library once before, on a routine visit to introduce herself, and it had seemed like a normal, if grand, public library. Therefore, she had been surprised to receive a call from Raphael that morning.

'Can I interest you in dealing with a small knowledge

emergency, if you're not busy?' he had asked. 'I'd attend to it myself, but I have . . . things to do.'

Jemma lowered her handset and surveyed the interior of the Friendly Bookshop. There was precisely one customer, being looked after by Maddy. 'Maddy can deal with everyone in the bookshop at present.' Maddy did an exaggerated thumbs-up at her while the customer's attention was elsewhere. 'Just tell me the address and what grade of emergency it is, and I'll be on my way.'

'It's at Charing Cross Library, and it's been reported as a Grade Four,' said Raphael. 'You could take Luke with you. It's a learning opportunity, and you never know when these sorts of skills will come in handy.'

'Oh.' In her few months as an Assistant Keeper Jemma had handled various levels of emergency, with effects ranging from mild unease to shaking floors, dimming lights, and threatened spontaneous combustion. However, she had never had to do so with someone in tow. 'Are you sure that's safe?'

'It's a Grade Four,' said Raphael. 'Everything will be fine, and it's just down the road. You can always send Luke back if he gets in your way.'

Jemma held in a sigh. 'Do I have a choice?'

Raphael said nothing.

'In that case, I'll be round in a few minutes.' She ended the call and took her kitbag from its cubbyhole under the counter.

And now here they were, looking up at the handsome four-storey building with its beautiful arched windows. 'Shall we go in?' said Luke, grinning.

'In a moment,' said Jemma. 'I'm checking for external effects.' She took a deep breath. 'I think it's safe. Come on, let's go in.'

They entered the library, which was exactly as Jemma had remembered: its ceiling as high, its carpet as blue, its staircase and balustrade as graceful. The worried expression on the librarian's face, however, was new. 'Jemma?' She extended a hand. 'I'm so glad you could come and help us in Raphael's absence.' She cast a doubtful glance at Luke, who was head to toe in black and particularly Gothic. She herself was willowy and pale, with long dark hair falling almost to her waist.

'This is Luke Varney, Raphael's assistant,' said Jemma. 'He's observing. Luke, this is Rebecca Sansom, the librarian here.'

'Pleased to meet you,' said Luke, and offered a long, pale hand. Rebecca hesitated a moment before shaking it.

'Can you tell us what the problem is?' asked Jemma. 'Raphael did give me an outline, but it's best to hear it in your own words.' As Rebecca was considering how to begin, Jemma wondered why Raphael had said that he was absent, rather than busy.

'It may be nothing,' said Rebecca, 'but one of our regulars came to the desk and told me that a book had been put in the wrong place. It was in the children's library, and she said it didn't look like a children's book at all.'

She paused. 'I was dealing with a customer at the time and I asked if she could bring me the book. She absolutely refused, saying it wasn't her job and she wouldn't touch it. She's normally very obliging, so that was decidedly odd.

Then she left shortly afterwards without borrowing anything, which is also unusual.'

'It is, rather,' said Jemma. 'Is the book still there, or have you removed it?'

Rebecca looked embarrassed. 'I'm probably being silly – maybe her attitude has affected me – but I didn't want to. I knew exactly which book she meant, but the closer I got, the odder I felt. As if I'd be doing something wrong by moving it, or even touching it.' She shook her head impatiently. 'I can't explain it. It's never happened before.'

Jemma and Luke exchanged glances. 'Is this a Grade Four emergency, Jemma?' Luke asked.

'Hard to say,' said Jemma. 'But I'm glad we have two full kits with us.' She held up her bag and Rebecca took a tiny step back. 'Could you point out the book to us, please?'

'Of course.' Rebecca took a deep breath. 'Follow me.'

The book wouldn't have been hard to find even without Rebecca's help. The children's library was busy with mothers, a few fathers, toddlers, and prams parked at all angles, but there was a clear semicircle of carpet into which no one ventured.

'There it is,' said Rebecca, pointing to the chapter books. On the top shelf Jemma saw a smallish book bound in tatty maroon leather. The spine was peeling, but she could make out the word *Ephemera* stamped on the spine in gilt letters.

She rummaged in her bag and produced a mask and a pair of tongs. 'Luke, can you be ready with a medium-sized book box and a chain, please.'

'Do you want me to come with you?' asked Luke.

Jemma was tempted to tell him that he should stay well back, away from any possible effects, but then reminded herself that it wasn't his fault she hated being watched. 'If you put a mask on, you can come as close as you like.'

'Excellent.' He took a mask from the bag and put it on, then took out a lead-lined book box. 'I can't smell or feel anything, can you?'

'We're out of range at the moment,' said Jemma. 'Are you ready?'

Luke nodded, and Jemma held up the tongs. 'In that case, we're going in.'

She walked forwards slowly, barely noticing Luke at her side. She was too busy repeating *I am an Assistant Keeper and you don't scare me* over and over in her head. Like Luke, she wasn't experiencing any particular discomfort. *Perhaps it's because I spend a lot of my time around unruly books*, she thought. *I suppose that would raise your tolerance.*

She took another step closer. *Could* it be a children's book? It was an odd title, certainly, and the book could use some repair, but that didn't mean it shouldn't be there. 'I need to look at it to be sure,' she said aloud, and took another step forward. Then she realised she was on her own. 'Are you OK, Luke?'

When she turned, Luke wore a puzzled frown. 'I think so, but I see what Rebecca means. It's a funny feeling, isn't it? Should I try another step forward?'

'Why not,' said Jemma. 'You can always step back.'

Luke took a determined step forward, then shivered. 'Oooh.'

Jemma could feel herself being observed, not just by Luke and Rebecca, but by the parents and toddlers, who had all stopped what they were doing. 'Let's get this done,' she said firmly, and took two steps forward before she changed her mind. Now that she was close to the book, she saw that it was steaming gently, like a horse after a gallop.

She made ready with her tongs. 'Box, please, Luke.'

'Forceps? Scalpel?' There was a distinct wobble in Luke's voice.

Jemma fought the urge to giggle. 'Not this time.' The book was sticking out slightly from its neighbours on the shelf. The last thing she wanted to do was touch it. She saw her hand shaking, and willed it to stop. She seemed to be looking at the book through a fine mist.

I am an Assistant Keeper and you don't scare me, she thought. Then she grabbed the book with the tongs and pulled it from the shelf. Her grip was fierce, and she hoped she wasn't damaging the book or causing it any pain. But needs must.

Luke held the box at arm's-length and Jemma fitted the book in. He slammed the box closed, then reached into his pocket and pulled out the silver chain, wincing as he did so.

'Sorry,' said Jemma. 'Do you want me to do this bit?'

'It's fine.' Luke set his teeth as he wound the chain around the box as if he were tying a parcel, then snapped the padlock closed.

And suddenly, everything was normal. Luke handed the

box to Jemma and she stowed it in her bag. They removed their masks and went back to the issue desk, where Rebecca was smiling for the first time since their arrival.

'Thank you so much,' she said. 'It feels better already. I thought we might have to cancel story time, but—' She eyed the children's section. 'You don't think there'll be any lasting effects, do you?'

'I wouldn't have thought so,' said Jemma. 'That was pretty straightforward.' Rebecca gave her an incredulous look. 'We'll take the book and examine it, and if there may be further problems, we'll get in touch.'

Rebecca leaned forward and lowered her voice. 'What shall I say if anyone asks me what that was about?'

'Completely up to you,' said Jemma. 'You could tell them that some old books release vapours and require removal, or that we're rehearsing a performance piece, or conducting a psychological experiment on inducing revulsion in strangers.'

'Ooh, yes,' said Rebecca. 'Would you like a cup of tea? I've got biscuits.'

Luke had a distinct gleam in his eye, and Jemma suspected he was hungry for something more substantial than biscuits. 'It's lovely of you to offer, but we ought to get back to headquarters and check out this book.' She hefted her bag. 'Hope the rest of your day is calm.'

'Me too,' said Rebecca. 'Nice to meet you, Luke.'

'And you,' said Luke, with a grin which showed his long canines. Rebecca smiled uncertainly in response.

'Easy, tiger,' said Jemma, as they walked down Charing Cross Road. 'You look as if you need some raw meat.'

Luke's cheeks turned pale pink, which was as close as he ever got to a full-on blush. 'I can't help it; it's an adrenaline thing. Fight or flight, you know.'

Not really, thought Jemma. 'Did you enjoy that?' she asked, to change the subject.

'Yes, mostly,' said Luke. 'I wasn't keen on the wobbly feeling, though. It made me doubt myself. I'm glad you were there to take care of things.'

'Oh, I feel like that a lot of the time,' said Jemma. 'It was slightly worse than usual, that's all.' The book was surprisingly heavy in her bag. She glanced at Luke to find him staring at her. 'What?'

'Why would you feel like that?' said Luke. 'You're really capable.'

'Mmm.'

'You are!' He gave her a gentle punch on the arm. 'Silly person.'

She laughed. 'So what else do you have planned for this morning, Luke?'

That gleam again. 'I assume you'll call in at the Friendly Bookshop first, so I thought I'd hang around and chat to Maddy.'

'What a surprise,' said Jemma. 'But yeah, why not. We've been quick, and there's supplies for you in the fridge if you need them.' *Besides, I don't want to walk in on Raphael being busy. Whatever that means.* The uncertain feeling came over her, but she brushed it away. *Luke's right. I'm a silly person.*

Chapter 2

When Jemma opened the door of the Friendly Bookshop Maddy was alone, sitting at the counter absorbed in a thick novel. She looked up, put in a bookmark, and closed the book. 'It's been quiet,' she said, sounding defensive.

'I'm not surprised,' said Jemma. 'It's a Tuesday morning in January. I'm not expecting any Valentine's Day shoppers until the weekend, and not too many of those.' She had done her best, with a window display of red hearts, paper roses, and an assortment of love stories and poetry anthologies, but she was a realist. 'How has Luna been?' She eyed Luna's bookshop bed. Luna was curled in a tight black ball, her back emphatically to the world. Folio balanced on the cushioned edge of the basket, amber eyes watchful.

'She hasn't been sick,' said Maddy, 'but she isn't very lively. Maybe we could try her with dry food later.'

'That's a good idea,' said Jemma, crouching by the basket and stroking Luna's soft black fur. 'Is Folio looking after you?'

Folio gave an affirmative chirp.

'That's a good cat.' She tickled him under his chin and he purred, tilting his head for maximum rubbing capacity. 'If she isn't better tomorrow, I'll ring the vet.' *Hopefully it's nothing*, she thought. Luna was a normal cat in most respects, but she also had some unusual abilities which Jemma hoped she wouldn't demonstrate to the vet.

She straightened up. 'Anyway, I'd better examine this book. I'll be in the stockroom; I shouldn't be more than ten or fifteen minutes.' She always gave a time when checking any new acquisition. Not because she was convinced something bad would happen, but you could never be too sure.

'Oh, what was it like?' asked Maddy.

'I can tell you all about it,' said Luke, leaning on the counter. 'Let us know if you need anything, Jemma.'

'Thanks so much,' Jemma replied, feeling thoroughly dismissed. She went through to the stockroom with her bag, switched on the light, and closed the door.

She put on a pair of white cotton gloves, a mask, and the Perspex goggles that hung on a peg by the door. It wasn't that the book had grown more dangerous since leaving Charing Cross Library, but in the stockroom, near other interesting and sometimes volatile books, an unexpected reaction might occur.

She put the book box on the little table, sat down, and took out her ring of tiny silver keys. 'Looks like a 3F,' she muttered, and soon discovered that she was right, which gave her a disproportionate sense of pleasure. She tutted at herself before opening the padlock and unwinding the chain. Her heart beat faster, as it did every time she inspected a problematic book. *Calm down*, she told herself. *You're an Assistant Keeper. This is your job.* She bit her lip, and eased open the lid of the lead-lined box.

Nothing happened. *Of course it didn't,* thought Jemma. *It's a Grade Four problem. The poor book is probably exhausted.* She touched the book with a gloved finger. It was at room temperature, and the steaming and hazing had vanished. Now that she had time to look at it properly, the book seemed more an object of pity than fear. Its once-handsome bindings were stained, the stitching coming apart at the bottom corner, and the gold lettering mostly worn away. Jemma had to peer to read the title: *Ephemera From A Life Of Transformation.*

Does that mean...? She lifted the book carefully from the box and opened it a little way. The first thing she saw was a picture of a wolf howling at a full moon. Jemma closed the book hurriedly, replaced it in the box, and chained it up. *There's no way I can take this to Burns Books. Not a shifter book.* Leaving the box on the table, she opened the stockroom door and stuck her head out. 'Maddy, what's our quietest section in the stockroom?'

After what sounded like scuffling, Maddy called back, 'There's P5, which is pet care.'

Absolutely not. 'What's the next quietest?'

'Corporate finance is pretty empty. Remember that guy who came in and bought nearly a shelf full of books the other week?'

'That'll do,' said Jemma. 'That's F3, isn't it?'

'Yes,' said Maddy, in what was almost a gasp.

Jemma found F3, which was rather bare, and laid the book box flat on the shelf. 'Behave yourself,' she told it sternly, then removed her protective gear and left, locking the stockroom door.

When she re-entered the main shop, Maddy was rearranging a shelf in the corner. Luke was leaning on the counter, arms folded, looking extremely pleased with himself. Jemma sighed. 'I'm perfectly aware that you two are going out. Just not in front of the customers, if you don't mind.'

Luke gave her a lazy salute. 'Yes, boss.' Jemma's eyes narrowed, but she couldn't exactly pull him up for agreeing with her.

'I suppose you'll head to Burns Books,' said Maddy, still facing the bookshelves.

'Um, yes.' *Not that you're keen for me to leave or anything.* 'I'll pop over and let Raphael know how it went. Then I imagine you'll want your lunch, Maddy.'

'Maybe I want my lunch too,' said Luke, and Maddy giggled. *You're like a pair of teenagers.*

Maddy reached up to a higher shelf and her hair fell back, exposing her neck.

'Luke, why don't you go on ahead?' said Jemma. 'I want to ask Maddy about this morning's sales.'

Luke shrugged. 'OK, see you in a minute,' he said, and ambled out.

Jemma walked over to her assistant. 'Maddy, that isn't a love bite, is it?'

Maddy jumped as if she had been shot and put a hand to her neck. 'He's very careful,' she said. 'He never draws blood.'

'I should hope not!' exclaimed Jemma. 'So this isn't the first time?'

A pink flush crept up Maddy's neck. *At least that means she's got plenty of blood left.* 'Maddy, look at me. How can you be so foolish? Do you know what it'll mean if he bites you properly? You can't let him do it. Think of the consequences.'

Maddy kept her face turned away. The skin on her neck was unbroken, but the bruise was darkening. 'Maybe I want him to,' she whispered.

Not for the first time, Jemma wished that Burns Books and the Friendly Bookshop employed normal shop assistants. They might arrive late, stretch out their breaks and ring in sick every so often, but at least she wouldn't have to worry about their immortal souls. 'I'm not going to lecture you, Maddy,' she said. 'You're a grown woman, and you're responsible for yourself.'

'Yes,' said Maddy, although she didn't seem too sure.

'Just be careful,' said Jemma. 'Luke's a vampire, with certain needs which he generally keeps in check, but he's only—' She had been about to say *human*. 'What's intended as harmless fun could get out of hand.'

Maddy sighed, drew her hair over her shoulder, and swapped a couple of books round on the shelf. 'Customers, eh,' she said, with a wry curl of her mouth. She glanced outside. 'Luke's waiting for you,' she said. Then she looked at Jemma properly. 'Aren't you taking the book you collected?'

'It's safer here,' said Jemma. She went back to the

counter, scribbled on a Post-it note, and gave it to Maddy. 'Here's the title and the shelf location. Could you put it on the database for me?'

'Of course.' Maddy's eyes widened as she read what Jemma had written. 'I'll get that done now.'

'Thanks. I'll be quick.' Jemma left her bag as a sort of guarantee and walked outside. Luke was leaning against a lamp post, hands in pockets. *You're doing a lot of leaning at the moment*, thought Jemma. She wasn't keen on that.

He unpeeled himself and they began to walk the short distance to Burns Books. She had to hurry to keep up with Luke's long, loping stride. 'Where's the book?' he asked.

'Staying at the Friendly Bookshop,' Jemma replied. Luke raised his eyebrows, but made no comment. *He knows.*

'I suppose you saw,' he ventured, a minute later.

Jemma swallowed. 'Yes, I did.'

He slowed down, as if to get the words in before they reached the other bookshop. 'To be honest, I don't know how I feel. I'm flattered, obviously, but it's a very big step. Mostly, becoming a vampire happens to you; you don't get to choose. So I don't know what it's like to have a choice.'

'Have you ever . . . done it before?'

Luke shook his head. 'Not to a human.' His eyes met Jemma's. 'It's lonely, you know, this life. Or it has been until now. I'm scared of what it means for Maddy, but also... I'd never have to lose her. We could be together always.'

They had reached the bookshop. Without another word, he pushed the door open, and they went in.

Chapter 3

'Thank heavens for that,' said Em, as soon as they entered. She was at the till ringing up books, with a long queue of customers waiting.

'Where's Raphael?' asked Luke, taking off his coat and joining her behind the counter.

'Have a nice day,' said Em, handing her customer a Burns Books paper bag with two books inside. 'Upstairs,' she said, out of the side of her mouth. 'He came into the café area two minutes after you both left and asked if I'd mind the shop for a few minutes while he saw to a small matter. Then he went up to his flat. That was an hour and a half ago.' She sighed.

'I'll take over,' said Luke. 'The customers downstairs will want lunch.'

'I've had customers wanting elevenses since ten thirty,' said Em, looking more put-upon than Jemma had ever seen her. 'If Raphael had said he'd take a while I wouldn't have minded, but—'

'Should my ears be burning?' enquired Raphael, as he

came into the main shop. 'Sorry, Em, it took longer than I thought.'

'It's OK,' said Em, with another sigh. 'I just wish you'd warned me.'

Raphael turned to Jemma. 'Everything all right at Charing Cross?'

'Yes, thanks,' Jemma replied. 'It was quite an easy one.' She studied Raphael. Something seemed different, but she couldn't have said what.

Luke snorted. 'If you say so, Jemma. I wouldn't have fancied being on my own with that book, personally.'

'Oh, you'll get used to it,' said Raphael. 'How's Luna? Any better?'

'I'll go downstairs and reopen the café then, shall I?' asked Em. She was still wearing her apron.

'Yes please, Em,' said Jemma. 'Thank you for stepping in and minding the shop at such short notice.'

Em smiled, her usual good humour restored. 'It was sort of fun, just a bit full-on. See you downstairs for a brew, maybe?' She walked briskly to the staircase leading to the lower floor, smoothing her hair though not one was out of place.

'Tea, what a good idea,' Raphael remarked as he watched Em go. 'Shall we adjourn downstairs, Jemma, and you can tell me about today's emergency. I trust you retrieved the book? May I see it?'

Behind Raphael, Luke's eyebrows shot up. Jemma gave him a warning glance. 'Let's have a quick chat,' she replied. 'I can't stay long; I need to relieve Maddy, and Luke would like an early lunch too.'

16

'Very well,' said Raphael, with a slight droop of the shoulders. 'Lead on, Macduff, as no one ever said.'

The huge basement of the shop was busy; it was easy to see where the queue of customers upstairs had come from. Customers were wandering from shelf to shelf, each in their own little world, occasionally adding to the books they held in their hands. Jemma sometimes wondered if a mild enchantment was cast over people when they entered the bookshop. If so, it certainly didn't harm their sales.

Em was getting things moving at the café counter, eyeing the queue forming in front of her. Jemma didn't have the heart to ask her for one more thing, especially after the morning she'd had. 'I'll make tea upstairs,' she said to Raphael. 'If you find us a table, I'll be down in a few minutes.'

'Marvellous,' said Raphael, and strode towards a table with two leather armchairs.

As she waited for the kettle to boil, Jemma pondered how to broach the topic of the troublesome book. Would Raphael be offended that she had judged it unsafe to bring it to Burns Books?

At last the kettle pinged, and she filled two bone-china mugs. *It isn't your fault*, she told herself. *Just be honest. Anyway, better to be cautious than not.* Even so, her heart grew heavier as she descended the stairs.

While she had been away Raphael had raided the nearest shelf, and was engrossed in *Old Baggage*. Jemma waved his mug above the book, which made him emerge. 'Thank you.' He took a swig of the scalding tea. 'This is most welcome. I imagine it is for you too; knowledge emergencies always make me thirsty. Although I suppose you had tea with Rebecca at the library.'

'No, we didn't stay,' said Jemma. 'Luke was . . . hungry.'

Raphael's eyebrows climbed up his forehead. 'Hungry, eh? Was that in response to the emergency, perhaps?'

Jemma shrugged. 'I think so.'

'Oh dear.' Raphael sipped reflectively. 'You'll have to watch out for that, especially if he does any solo work.'

'Solo work?' Jemma stared at her boss. 'Luke's been out with me once as an observer. It isn't appropriate for him to go solo to a knowledge emergency yet. Or for some time.' She remembered how Luke had hung back in the library, which had been perfectly understandable.

'I don't mean right now,' said Raphael, in the soothing voice which Jemma found particularly annoying. 'In the future, of course.' He drank more tea. 'I assume it was the usual roaring success. Did you bring the book?'

Here we go. 'I decided it was best to keep it at the Friendly Bookshop,' she said. 'It appears to be a book about . . . transformation.'

Raphael flinched, then gazed into the depths of his mug. 'Probably wise,' he said at last. 'So, are you ready for tomorrow's interviews in Berkshire?'

'Yes, I think so,' said Jemma, caught off guard by the change of subject. 'I've printed three copies of the job description, person specification, assessment matrix and question sheets. They're in three folders back at my shop, along with the interviewees' application forms.' *Luke and Em will probably start a mutiny when they hear that*

Raphael and I are out for most of tomorrow, she thought. *Especially after today.* 'Are you sure you need me, though? It seems odd for me to be recruiting an Assistant Keeper when I've only been one myself for five minutes.'

'Think of what you've seen,' said Raphael. 'Think of all you've done. You may not have been in post long, but you've seen more than some Keepers who have worked for me for decades.' He stretched out his long legs. 'Besides, it will be good for your development, and a chance to meet another senior member of the Keepers' Guild.'

'Oh yes,' said Jemma. 'Who is it? It would be nice to put a name to the face.' In reality, she was desperate to Google this mysterious senior Keeper so that she could feel at least slightly prepared. Then again, if Raphael's online presence was anything to go by, they would be notable by their absence from the internet.

'Hold your horses, you'll meet him tomorrow,' said Raphael.

So this Keeper's a he. That's a start.

'You'll enjoy the interviews,' said Raphael. 'After all, management things are your speciality. I dare say he'll be impressed with you.' He sipped his tea, and as he did so regarded Jemma with an appraising look that made her slightly uncomfortable. 'Tell me, Jemma, would you consider taking on any more responsibilities?'

'Me?' said Jemma. 'More responsibilities? But I'm still learning.' That hadn't come out right, and her face flushed hot. 'I mean, thank you for your faith in me, but I've got the bookshop to run, committees to administer, emergencies to deal with, and you've just mentioned training Luke. I'm not sure I can fit any more in.' She sipped her own tea while considering how to phrase her next words. 'There are days when I feel as if I'm reading the manual to work out my next move.'

'But not many days,' said Raphael.

'Not as many as when I first started, no,' said Jemma. 'But enough. I'd rather be completely confident in what I'm doing before taking on any more.'

Raphael laughed. 'That's my cautious deputy.' He drained his mug. 'Anyway, I had better head upstairs and take over from Luke. Especially if he's hungry.' One eyebrow quirked slightly, then he stood up. 'I'll see you here bright and early tomorrow for our jaunt. Cinnamon rolls and coffee are on me.' He slipped *Old Baggage* into his pocket and strode away.

Jemma looked towards the café counter, hoping for a few minutes' chat with Em, but that would be impossible. Em was busy serving customers, warming paninis, making drinks and ringing up sales. *Maybe I can pop in after the rush. I'd better go, too, or Maddy's lunch will be delayed.*

She thought of Luke and Maddy out to lunch together, walking in a park or a square, perhaps heading into a quiet corner and— She rose abruptly and took the empty mugs to the counter. *They're grown-ups. They both know what they're doing. Or they should.*

Her stomach rumbled. *At least if it's quiet at the Friendly Bookshop I can eat my lunch in peace...* She made her way through the meandering customers to the great oak door and headed upstairs, concentrating on the lunch waiting for her back at the shop: a pastrami sandwich on rye bread, with Swiss cheese, mustard, and a dill pickle.

It was only when she was halfway to the Friendly Bookshop that she realised what had puzzled her about Raphael. Usually his clothes clashed with rather than complemented each other, but today he had been soberly dressed in a navy suit with a white shirt and a grey tie – and she was certain he hadn't been wearing those clothes when she had arrived to collect Luke. And now she thought of it, he had said nothing about what he had been doing in his flat for so long. *Maybe I can find out tomorrow*, she thought, and pushed it to the back of her mind. Or she tried; the thought resurfaced throughout the afternoon, popping up like a bubble in expensive wallpaper that wouldn't smooth out.

Chapter 4

'Not far now,' said Raphael, indicating left. Gertrude the camper van ticked reassuringly, like a large friendly clock. 'You're very quiet, Jemma. Are you all right?'

'Yes, fine,' said Jemma automatically. 'I didn't sleep well. That's probably it.'

'Things on your mind?' Raphael glanced at her. 'If I didn't know better, I'd wonder if you were carsick. You haven't even had a cinnamon roll.'

'It's not long since breakfast,' Jemma replied. *You're being silly*, she told herself. *It's probably nothing. You're imagining stuff.*

That wasn't what you were telling yourself last night, said the annoying little voice in her head, which had a habit of surfacing at the worst times. *You were convinced something was wrong.*

That was different, countered Jemma. *And that's unfair. What you think on your own in the middle of the night and what you think in broad daylight are two different things.*

She had been looking forward to talking things over

with Carl the previous evening, but he had texted at half past four to say that he was staying at his mum's that night. *Unexpected early meeting*, he had written. *Got prep to do. I'll fill you in later, if it comes off. Love you x*

And with that Jemma had had to be content. She had made herself a bowl of soup, as she was still full from her pastrami sandwich, and settled to read through the interviewees' application forms for the next day. However, Raphael, in his uncharacteristically coordinated outfit, kept getting in the way.

What had he been doing upstairs? It had obviously involved an online meeting, since he'd dressed up. Presumably, as he had conducted the meeting in his own flat, he didn't want either the customers or Em to know about it. *Or Luke*, thought Jemma. *That's why Raphael asked me to take him, even though it meant leaving the shop understaffed.* And leaving Em, who had no specific training, in sole charge of a volatile bookshop was a reckless move.

'What were you doing yesterday morning?' she blurted, before she could stop herself.

Raphael chuckled. 'I wondered when you'd ask me that,' he said. 'Let's get through today first.'

'Aren't we going to Windsor?' said Jemma, as he took an unanticipated exit at the roundabout.

'Not this time,' said Raphael. 'If we were interviewing at Drusilla's ex-bookshop, maybe. I'd rather not go there, for obvious reasons. There may still be something of Drusilla lingering on the premises.'

Jemma shivered. Drusilla Davenport, former Assistant

Keeper for Berkshire and intellectual snob, had done her best to destroy Raphael's bookshop and remove him from his position as Keeper for England. However, Jemma, with considerable help from the rest of the team, had managed to thwart her and send her packing to who knew where. 'Did we ever find out who bought her bookshop?'

'Yes,' Raphael replied, his eyes for once on the road. 'It was sold as a going concern, with most of the stock, to a company which already has a few bookshops in the south-east. I imagine they were more than happy to get a footing in Windsor.'

'Normal bookshops?' asked Jemma. 'Not magical ones?'

'Completely normal, as far as I know,' said Raphael. 'I popped into the bookshop when I was passing one day, and discovered that it was a well-arranged, attractive book emporium with no bad habits.'

'What were the staff like? Did you meet the manager?'

'I did,' said Raphael. 'Remember your old friend Marcus who interviewed for the assistant's job with us?'

'No!' exclaimed Jemma, grinning from ear to ear. 'Really?'

'Oh yes. He's very proud of his shop and plans to make it the talk of the Home Counties. The staff are the usual mix of studenty types with writing aspirations and staff from other bookshops who are helping Marcus get established.'

'I'm glad Marcus is doing well,' said Jemma, and meant it, though she was also secretly glad that Marcus would be too busy to sniff around Burns Books any more.

Raphael made another turn, and soon they were in the outskirts of a town. 'We're interviewing candidates in the reading room of the town library.' Jemma reflected on how odd it was that she hadn't known where they were going. Normally she would have been the one to send out the letters, or at least arrange the venue. Presumably the mysterious senior Keeper or his admin team had performed that function.

'How many do we have today?' asked Raphael.

'Four,' said Jemma. 'The only one I know is Hermione Dawes.' She had been surprised that Hermione had applied for the post: she had seemed contented with her role in north London. 'Do you know why she's gone for it?'

'I don't,' said Raphael, 'but she'd be a good appointment. We'll ask at the interview. But now we'd better stop talking; this one-way system confuses me no end.'

Twenty minutes later they were welcomed by a beaming librarian, signed in at the desk, and handed badges. 'I'll take you to the reading room,' she said, 'and then you can settle in with the other gentleman.'

'Oh, he's here, is he?' said Raphael. 'Jolly good.' And he waved Jemma forward before she had a chance to consult the names in the visitors' book.

Their footsteps echoed on the parquet floor. Surreptitiously, Jemma straightened her necklace, checked she was still wearing both her earrings, and made sure her blouse was sitting straight. Raphael nudged her. 'You don't need to worry,' he said. Jemma wasn't sure whether to believe him, since he was wearing comparatively sensible clothing, a turquoise bow tie the only splash of colour.

'Here we are,' said the librarian, and opened the door with a flourish.

The reading room was beautiful, with tall shelves between its large, many-paned windows. At the end of the room was a raised platform, on which stood a large rectangular table with three chairs on one side and one on the other.

But Jemma only had eyes for the man sitting in the middle chair. He seemed tall even sitting down, with broad shoulders and dark hair greying at the temples. He stood up as they walked closer, and unleashed a charming smile. His eyes were sea green, and he wore a beautifully cut grey suit with a white shirt and a tie that matched his eyes.

Gosh, thought Jemma.

'Lennox, good to see you,' said Raphael, walking forward with his hand outstretched. As they pumped hands, he turned to Jemma. 'Lennox, this is my deputy, Jemma James. Jemma, this is Dr Lennox Nash.'

***

'I still think Hermione is the right person for the role,' said Jemma. She kept her voice light and pleasant, but inside she wanted to kick the table leg.

'I have to say, Lennox, I don't disagree,' said Raphael. 'She scored well on knowledge, she is already an Assistant Keeper, and she has a good reason for moving to Berkshire.'

'I'm not sure how she'd fit in,' said Lennox smoothly. 'She'd be too much of a shock after Drusilla.'

'I've met Drusilla,' said Jemma. 'Is someone different a

bad choice?'

Lennox Nash flashed his charming smile again. 'I in no way condone Drusilla's activities, Jemma. However, Drusilla was very popular among the literary circles in Berkshire and further afield. Serving on the committees of literary festivals, advising the local university press, making book recommendations on local radio.' He laughed. 'I can't see Hermione doing much of that.'

'At least she won't be endangering the Keepers' Guild by attempting to murder her boss,' Jemma shot back.

The smile vanished. 'If we have to say "at least" about a candidate, they cannot be the best choice.' He inspected his fingernails in a weary manner.

'Who is everyone's second choice?' asked Raphael. 'I liked the first candidate, Sarah. She's been an Under Keeper in the university archives for ten years, she understands the maintenance and preservation of old and rare books, and she's ready for more responsibility now that her children have left home. She would be a safe pair of hands.'

'I agree,' said Jemma. She would much rather have appointed Hermione, but better safe, slightly dull Sarah than the awful braggart who had tried to hand her his coat when she opened the door to call him in.

'I must say that I preferred Ben,' said Lennox Nash.

You would, thought Jemma sourly.

'We clicked, rather. He is less experienced, certainly, but a personable fellow who will go far.'

'I didn't take to him,' said Raphael, and Jemma could have cheered.

Lennox made a show of shuffling his papers together. 'As the other candidate couldn't make it today, we have a result. Sarah it is. Will you phone her, Raphael, or shall I?'

'As head of the panel, I suppose it's my job,' said Raphael, and Jemma blinked. She had never seen Raphael volunteer for an administrative or managerial task before.

'Pity it's taken so long to fill the post,' said Lennox. 'Not so long ago we'd have used the grapevine and had a new Assistant Keeper by the end of the week.'

'Which may explain how Drusilla slipped through the net,' said Raphael. 'I was hesitant about this new system, but now I think it improves equality and opens up opportunities for people who would have been overlooked in what many would call the bad old days.'

'Mm.' Lennox gave his papers a final tap on the table, then squared them off and handed them to Raphael. 'I'd take you both out to lunch, but I'm giving a guest lecture at seven and I haven't got round to writing it yet.' A flash of white teeth. 'Nice to meet you, Jemma.' His handshake was very firm, but without warmth. 'Till we meet again.' He draped his long grey coat over his arm and strolled to the door with the air of a man who had places to go and people to see.

***

Over lunch, and for most of the journey back, Raphael had filled her in on Lennox Nash's background. Top of his year at university (1842), a noted bibliophile and scholar, he had chosen to give up his fame and reputation to retreat into the obscurity of an Under Keepership abroad before rising to his present heights.

'If he's so famous,' said Jemma, 'how come no one's realised he's been around for such a long time?'

'Oh, Jemma,' said Raphael, like an indulgent uncle. 'He told people that the original Lennox Nash was his great-grandfather. Anyway, look at him. Does he appear two hundred years old?'

'Not exactly,' said Jemma. By any measure, Lennox was a handsome man. *So why can't I take to him, when everyone else finds him irresistible?* 'When did you get to know him?'

'Oh, we ran into each other in Paris some years ago,' said Raphael. 'I was just visiting, but Lennox was handling rather a delicate matter for the then head of the Guild.' He changed lanes at high speed, and Jemma's stomach lurched in response. To cheer herself up after the interviews she had treated herself to a rich lunch, but now she was paying the penalty. 'If Lennox had given all his attention to his Keeper duties, rather than splitting himself between those, scholarship, and celebrity, he would probably be head of the Guild now.'

'Maybe,' said Jemma. 'I still think we should have appointed Hermione. She was the best candidate, and you know it.'

'Perhaps we should trust Lennox's judgement,' said Raphael. 'He's very intelligent. Very wise.'

Jemma said nothing. Instead, she took her phone from her bag and checked it for messages. Two from Maddy and three from Luke, all saying that things were running smoothly at the bookshops. Nothing from Carl. She put her phone away and glanced at Raphael. 'I wasn't sure what to make of him,' she said.

She expected Raphael to ask her why that was, but instead Gertrude shot forward and the back of Jemma's head embedded itself in the headrest. They had never gone so fast. 'This doesn't feel safe,' she groaned.

'Perfectly safe,' said Raphael. 'I hadn't seen how late it was. I must sort out Sarah's paperwork, and you'll want to get back to your bookshop before Maddy closes up.'

Jemma checked the clock on the dashboard. 'It's a quarter to three, Raphael,' she said. 'I thought we were going to discuss, you know, the other thing.'

Raphael kept his eyes on the road. 'We'll pick that up tomorrow when you come to Burns Books. I assume you are coming? Or would you rather skip this week, since you haven't spent much time in your own shop?'

'Oh no, I'll come,' said Jemma, and clenched her teeth as Raphael changed lanes. She had been suspicious that something was going on before. Now she was certain, and she had no intention of missing the opportunity to find out what it was.

Chapter 5

'Am I imagining things?' Jemma asked Maddy, as they made tea in the back room of the Friendly Bookshop on Thursday morning. She had already surreptitiously inspected Maddy's neck, which to her relief appeared wound-free.

Maddy squashed her teabag against the side of her mug. 'I don't think so, but it's hard to know without having seen any of it myself. It isn't like Raphael to be secretive.'

'That's what worries me,' said Jemma. 'It's more like him to tell me much more than I need to know. Right now it feels as if he's keeping things from me.'

'Well, from what you've said, you'll find out today,' said Maddy. 'And you're due at Burns Books in ten minutes. What does Carl think?'

'We haven't had a chance to discuss it.' They hadn't. She had gone upstairs to her flat the day before, bursting to vent to him, but when her phone had rung at half past five and she saw Carl's name flash up, she guessed this would not be a good time.

She answered it. 'Hi. How did it go?'

'Good, I think. I've just got out.'

Jemma frowned. 'I thought it was an early meeting.'

'It was, but they asked if I could meet with more people that afternoon, so I was prepping for that. I haven't stopped all day.'

'Prepping for what?'

A pause. 'I don't want to talk about it much in case it doesn't come off. It's to do with taking *A New Leaf* outside London.'

'Wow, really?' *A New Leaf* was Carl's first play, which he had written while working as the barista at Burns Books. It had premiered in the lower floor of the bookshop, a drama critic had reviewed it, and it had been picked up for a short run at a local theatre. 'Who would have thought, when you were working on your play in the evenings, that it would go so far? That's brilliant news!'

'Thanks. If it happens.' He sounded dismissive, which was a sure sign that this opportunity, whatever it was, meant a lot to him.

'I'm sure it will. It got great reviews.'

'Keep your fingers crossed for it. And me.'

'So where are you now?'

He half-smothered a yawn. 'At Mum's, because it's nearest. I'm sorry, but I couldn't face the tube journey. I'm absolutely shattered, and I've got to do it again tomorrow.'

'Why? Haven't you had all the meetings?'

A short, mirthless laugh. 'I thought so, but they've asked me to pitch my new play.'

'But you're still writing it.'

'That's the problem. I'm sitting at my laptop, writing a synopsis and getting a couple of scenes polished for tomorrow. Mum is cooking jerk chicken, rice and peas for me, bless her.'

'Oh, that's good.' Jemma loved cooking, but she would never have dared to attempt that dish; Carl's mum Debra would make a much better job of it. 'I'd better let you go, if you're working on stuff. Good luck for tomorrow.'

'Cheers, Jemma. Love you.'

'Love you—' But the phone went dead, and she wasn't sure whether Carl had heard her or not.

Jemma looked at the phone for a moment, then went to the kitchen bookshelf and found *Cooking For One*. She flicked through it and nothing appealed, so she settled for beans on toast and a mug of decaf tea. She had a feeling she would need all her sleep for the following day, and whatever Raphael had in store.

It's perfectly normal that Carl didn't ask me about my day, she thought, as Maddy gazed enquiringly at her. *His head's full of his plays, and no wonder. Whatever it is, it's a brilliant opportunity. Let's face it, interviewing people for a job miles away won't have any impact on him. Or me, really.* 'I'd better go down to Burns Books.' She poured her tea into a travel mug, then went through to the main shop and picked up her coat and bag. 'Wish me luck for whatever it is.'

'Good luck,' said Maddy. 'Hopefully you won't need it.' She didn't sound convinced.

'Ah, there you are,' said Raphael, as soon as she walked through the door of Burns Books. 'I was wondering when you would appear.'

'It's five to nine, Raphael,' said Jemma. 'I'm early.'

'I was earlier, and so was Luke.' Raphael sounded triumphant. 'You don't mind holding the fort for a little while, do you, Luke?'

'That's fine,' said Luke, his voice flat. 'So long as you're back before the rush.'

'Oh, we shall be,' said Raphael. 'This shouldn't take more than half an hour or so.' He glanced at Jemma. 'Ah, you've brought tea with you. Let's get started.' He walked towards the door that led to his flat.

Jemma stared at him, not moving. 'Aren't you having tea? Or coffee?'

'I've just had one. Come on, let's get going.'

'That doesn't usually stop you.' Raphael habitually consumed so much caffeine that seeing him without a cup or mug seemed unnatural.

Raphael opened the door and held it for her. 'Now, please, Jemma.' And she had no choice but to climb the stairs.

Raphael unlocked his flat door and took Jemma through to the sitting room, where she perched on a new stripy sofa which Giulia must have introduced. Raphael sat in the armchair opposite. The only comfort she could take from the situation was that he was dressed in his usual style, sporting blue and green plaid trousers, a maroon waistcoat, a pink dress shirt, and the purple bow tie with gold polka dots she had given him for Christmas. 'I assume Folio is at your bookshop. Is Luna better?'

'Yes, he is, and yes, she seems better. She's quiet, but

she hasn't been sick for a couple of days and she's eating dry food and drinking plenty of water.'

'Oh, that's positive.' Silence fell, and Raphael looked at his feet.

'I thought you wanted to get on?' said Jemma.

'Yes. Yes, I did.' Another pause. 'I'm sure you've noticed that I have been a little . . . absent lately.'

'Yes, I suppose I have.'

'Yes, well.' He studied the floor, his fingers knitted together and his thumbs circling each other, first one way, then the other. 'I've decided to take a bit of a break.'

'Like a holiday?' asked Jemma, though she had a pretty good idea that wasn't it.

'You could say that, but a working holiday.' He sighed. 'I spoke to Armand Dupont a few weeks ago, and told him that if I could take on work elsewhere for a short time, that would suit me very well. He said he'd see what he could do, and we had a meeting on Tuesday.'

'I see.' *That explains Tuesday morning.*

'Oh good,' said Raphael, brightening. 'I'm glad you don't mind.'

'I don't know if I mind or not yet,' said Jemma. 'How long will you be away?'

'Six months.' Jemma's mouth dropped open. 'Maybe a year. It depends on how much work there is to do.'

'Six months? You can't leave for six months, never mind a year! What will we do? What will the shop do?'

'The shop will be fine,' said Raphael, and the annoying soothing note was back. 'After all, you're the manager, Luke and Em will still be here, and you have Maddy at your shop, who's very reliable.'

Jemma took a few deep breaths. Whatever she had expected, this wasn't it. 'So where are you going? Will you come back at weekends?'

Raphael looked embarrassed. 'Not exactly. I'm going to Italy with Giulia. We're so wrapped up in our work that it will be nice to spend some time together.' He shot a furtive glance at Jemma. 'There's another reason, too.'

Jemma was tempted to tell him she didn't care. *How can he leave me alone with all this?* But she fought down her rising anger. 'What's the other reason?'

Raphael raised his head and met her eyes. 'I'm exhausted. I've had enough.' He raised one hand. It was steady for a few seconds, then began to tremble slightly. Raphael lowered it and gripped it with his other hand. 'This business with Drusilla has had an effect on me. Some of that is my own fault, because I gave in to the fascination with shifting which I had kept in check for many years. However, that was also necessary to bring about her downfall.'

'That book at Charing Cross Library…' Jemma studied him. 'Was that intentional? And if so, who put it there? Who brought it into the library? It couldn't be…'

Raphael lifted his hands, then let them fall. 'The difficulty is that we don't know. It could be a coincidence, although it would be interesting to see if there is a paper trail for that book. And while it's very unlikely that Drusilla would be able to manage the trick she tried in the London Library, it isn't impossible. We have no idea where she is.'

'But it must be impossible! Drusilla's out of the Guild and out of a job. She's mortal, and she's lost her powers.'

'Unlikely, but not impossible,' said Raphael.

'Will you be safe away from the bookshop?' asked Jemma. 'I mean, doesn't it give you protection?'

'It does,' said Raphael, 'but it also requires protection. In my present state, I fear that I would be unable to protect it from a serious, sustained attack.'

Jemma sighed, taking it all in. 'Well, at least you won't be going yet. I mean, there will be a recruitment process to replace you.'

Raphael said nothing.

'There would have to be an expression of interest, then interviews…' Jemma's voice faltered as Raphael remained silent. 'Wouldn't there?' Her voice cracked on the last words.

'That's all been taken care of,' said Raphael. 'Our tickets are booked, and Giulia and I are flying early on Saturday morning.' His expression was a curious mixture of guilt and numbness. 'I'm sorry, Jemma.'

Chapter 6

Raphael cleared his throat and Jemma stopped sweeping. 'Sorry to interrupt, Jemma, but Giulia and I are leaving in a minute.'

'Already?' said Jemma. 'Aren't you going to introduce your – the new Keeper?'

'I was, but he's just texted that he won't be here until five thirty at the earliest. Our taxi for the airport hotel will arrive in a few minutes.'

'Oh.' Jemma put the broom away in the back room and returned, resisting the urge to wipe her hands on her black trousers.

The last two days had been a whirlwind. After Raphael's bombshell she had, rather guiltily, abandoned the Friendly Bookshop to Maddy's care and spent most of her waking hours at Burns Books. She had checked that all the books in the stockroom were on the shop's database, and made sure the boxes were stacked neatly and the room clean. She had gone through the café's inventory with Em and sent a copy of their stock list to Tina, who would be running the main branch of Rolando's while Giulia was away, though she suspected Giulia would require regular updates. She had overhauled both floors of the bookshop, tidying, removing scruffy books, and generally putting its best face forward. She had cleaned, waxed, and polished till her arms ached, and made sure the shop's paperwork was in order.

Raphael, meanwhile, had been mostly absent.

In some ways that was understandable; he had spent time calling on the various booksellers who supplied the shop and saying his goodbyes. It also meant there was less opportunity for the shop to guess what was happening. Jemma suspected he had conducted all his sabbatical activities in his own flat, which was somehow immune from the bookshop's formidable powers for gleaning information. Perhaps he had cast a spell on it. At any rate, Jemma was glad that the shop remained calm, with a steady, pleasant temperature and no ominous rumblings.

When Raphael had broken the news to Jemma on Thursday morning, he had asked if she would mind informing Luke, Em, and Maddy. 'Take them out to lunch,' he had said. 'Maybe a drink after work. But not here.'

Jemma, not sure whether she was more angry or upset, was sorely tempted to go downstairs and announce it then and there; only the thought of the ensuing chaos stopped her. Instead, she took her staff to the Rat and Compasses that evening.

The deed done, they sat gloomily over their drinks. 'He can't,' said Maddy.

'He already has,' Jemma replied. That was enough to

stun them into silence.

A few lugubrious minutes later, Luke asked who would replace Raphael. 'I mean, someone has to.'

'Yes,' said Jemma. She remembered the conversation days before, when Raphael had asked whether she would like more responsibility and she had declined. *I wonder...* But now she would never know. *In any case, I'm not ready. I don't know if I'll ever be ready.*

'So who is it?' asked Em. 'Not you?'

Jemma shook her head. 'I don't know; I haven't asked.'

They stared at her. 'You haven't asked?'

Jemma turned her glass of red wine on its stem. 'No, I haven't. Raphael didn't tell me, and I didn't ask him.'

That, in itself, was perhaps the most disturbing thing of all. She couldn't remember a time when she hadn't wanted to *know*. She was a peeker at presents, a Googler, a prober. Nice people would call it curiosity, but Jemma knew she was nosy, and saw no shame in it. But this – this was different. She didn't want to know for sure, because she was pretty sure that she already knew.

After some muttering about how things wouldn't be the same without Raphael, and that they didn't know what the bookshops would make of it, everyone left. Jemma knew she should have made a speech, convinced them that things would be fine and that they must stick together and support the new Acting Keeper, whoever he was, but she didn't have the heart for it. Instead, she walked the short distance home, let herself in, and stroked Luna, who had come to meet her, indulging in a big stretch on the way.

'Hello, sweetheart,' she said.

'Hello,' said Carl's voice, and she nearly jumped out of her skin.

'I didn't think you'd be back yet,' she said, walking into the living room, where he was sprawled on the sofa reading a copy of *The Stage*. Her voice sounded accusing even to herself.

'Yeah. I haven't long got in. Delays on the tube, platforms shut... You know.'

Jemma knew; she had spent enough of her working life strap-hanging and waiting for connections on draughty platforms. 'How was it? Have you heard?' She couldn't tell from his expression, which was neutral. Then again, Carl was a trained actor. If he wanted to hide his feelings, he could.

He shook his head. 'Not yet. They said maybe tomorrow. So I guess I'm twiddling my thumbs.' Jemma remembered Raphael doing that in his living room that morning. It seemed as if a year had passed since then.

'Hopefully early tomorrow,' she said. 'Shall I ring for a pizza? I can't face cooking.'

Carl gazed at her as if seeing her for the first time. 'You look exhausted.' He swung his legs down and patted the sofa beside him. 'What's up?'

Jemma sat, and hesitated. She wasn't sure whether what she said in her flat would reach the bookshop. She hoped Brian, its former owner, had placed an insulating charm on the shop, because she was bursting to let it out. 'Raphael is going away,' she said.

Carl put an arm around her, and she buried her head in her hands. She longed to cry, but somehow, despite the lump in her throat, there were no tears. 'I've been at the pub, telling the team. They're in shock.'

'I bet they are,' said Carl. 'Do you want to talk about it?'

Jemma took a breath, and as she did, thought of Carl's two days of hard work and the uncertainty he was going through. Was it fair to dump this on him at the end of it? Maybe things wouldn't be so bad after all. Maybe the shop wouldn't mind the change. Maybe the Acting Keeper would turn out just fine.

'It's only for six months,' she said. 'I'm sure I'll be able to contact Raphael if I need anything. I'm probably catastrophising, like I always do.' Carl gave her a doubtful look. 'Maybe I should cook. There's mince in the fridge; I could make spaghetti bolognese.'

Carl grinned and kissed her. 'I was hoping you'd say that.' He levered himself off the sofa. 'I'll go find a bottle of red.'

'Thanks,' said Jemma, though her small glass of wine at the pub had tasted sour and musty. Perhaps it had been filtered through her anger and resentment. She got to her feet and dragged herself to the kitchen area, where Luna wound herself round her legs like a cat in the peak of health.

Friday at Burns Books had been just as hard. The heavy work was finished, but Luke and Em were both under a cloud, and her day had been punctuated by texts from Maddy.

I can't log in to the database.

Have you reorganised the stockroom? I can't find

anything.

One of the hearts on the Valentine's display has cracked.

My bookshop knows, thought Jemma. She replied to each text supportively, carefully, weighed down by guilt that she was putting her staff through this. *I don't have a choice. We just have to keep going.*

Raphael had forbidden them from making any sort of fuss over his departure or telling the customers. 'They'll find out soon enough,' he said. He had left his packing until Friday afternoon.

Privately, he had asked Jemma to care for Folio. 'He'll be fine,' he said. 'He's bonded with the bookshop, not me, although of course I'll miss him. He spends most of his time at your bookshop anyway, with Luna.'

'Yes,' said Jemma. 'He does.' She imagined what Folio would do when he saw the suitcases, and shivered.

But now it was time for goodbyes. Giulia stood beside Raphael, holding his arm and looking determined. *This must be strange for her too*, thought Jemma. *I wonder how she feels about leaving her business?* While they were friendly, she would never dream of asking Giulia such a personal question.

'I suppose this is it,' said Raphael. 'I'm not very good at this sort of thing, but it's been a pleasure working with you all. You're the best staff I've ever had in over three hundred years of bookselling. I shall miss you, but I'm sure you'll do a great job. Thank you.' He shook Luke's hand, then Em's.

As he shook Maddy's, Folio rushed in from the back

room, meowing as if his life depended on it, and launched himself at Raphael, rubbing his head against his legs.

'I haven't forgotten you,' said Raphael. He leaned down and stroked the cat's silky ears. 'I've stocked up on tins of salmon and bought extra treats,' he said to Jemma. 'They're in the cupboard in the back-room kitchen.'

Folio lifted his head and yowled. 'I'm sorry, Folio, but I have to go.'

'Povero gatto,' said Giulia. 'He doesn't understand.'

'Yes he does,' murmured Jemma.

With some difficulty, Raphael moved forwards and held out his hand to Jemma. 'I know you'll do me proud,' he said, and she wanted to cry.

He looked at her wrist. 'You're not wearing the bracelet I gave you. At Christmas, remember. Don't you like it?' He sounded matter-of-fact, not disappointed.

'It's too nice for every day,' said Jemma. 'Besides, I thought it might – do something.'

'There's no point in having nice things if you don't use them,' Raphael replied. 'Wear it anyway.'

Jemma nodded. *Why does that matter now?* she thought.

From behind the door to his flat, Raphael retrieved a laptop bag and a battered brown leather suitcase with brass fastenings. He put down the case to lock the door and Folio immediately leapt onto it, yowling.

A horn beeped outside and everyone jumped.

Raphael scooped the cat up, cuddling him and crooning. 'Jemma, would you mind holding Folio for a minute? I don't think he'll let us go otherwise.'

Jemma held out her arms and Raphael gently transferred Folio. He stopped yowling and looked at Raphael. His eyes, normally gold or light amber, were so dark brown that they were almost black. He burrowed his head into the crook of Jemma's elbow and lay still, apart from the agitated twitching at the tip of his tail.

'I'm sorry, Folio,' she whispered in his ear, rocking him gently.

'Ciao, everyone,' said Giulia. 'Stay strong.' She embraced them briskly. 'Time to go, caro mio.'

Raphael went to the door and opened it for her. The bell jangled merrily, as it always did. 'I shall miss you all very much,' he said. 'Everything will be fine.' He followed Giulia out of the shop, and closed the door behind them.

Once the noise of the bell had died away, Jemma realised she was still staring at the door as if something might happen. She walked to the window, but the taxi had already vanished. 'Shall I make tea?' she asked. 'There's no point in reopening the bookshops now.'

'I'll do it,' said Em, her voice flat. 'When's this new Keeper coming?'

'Not for another half hour,' said Jemma.

They trooped downstairs and sat round a large café table. Em made tea in the big teapot and brought it over with a milk jug and a bowl of sugar lumps. 'Might as well do it properly.'

They sat, drinking tea, saying nothing. Every so often Jemma glanced at Folio, who was curled in a tight ball on top of one of the bookshelves, facing away from them. 'Come on, everyone,' she said, putting her mug down. 'It's six months. We all know what we're doing. It'll be fine.'

'What's that?' asked Luke, looking at the great oak door. 'I could have sworn I heard footsteps.'

'You can't have,' Jemma replied. 'I locked the door when Raphael left. I didn't want Folio sneaking out and going after him—'

The door swung open with a flourish and the light shone full on Lennox Nash, resplendent in a navy three-piece suit and a caped overcoat and also wearing a charming smile. Then a furrow formed between his eyebrows.

'So you're the hard-working staff Raphael has told me so much about,' he said, and the smile disappeared.

Chapter 7

'We weren't expecting you just yet,' said Jemma. She realised how bad that sounded. 'I mean, we don't normally shut till at least five o'clock on a Friday, and often five thirty, but with Raphael leaving…'

'Get off all right, did he?' Lennox looked around him. 'I bet he couldn't wait to leave for sunny Italy.'

Jemma got to her feet. 'Everyone, this is Dr Lennox Nash. Lennox, meet Luke, Em, and Maddy. Luke is the assistant here, Em runs the café, and Maddy works for me at the Friendly Bookshop.'

He took them in, then strolled forward. 'Splendid, splendid.' The smile was back on his face. 'Wonderful to meet you.' He gazed into their faces as if committing them to memory. 'Luke.' As he pumped Luke's hand, his nose wrinkled slightly. 'So you're the assistant.'

'Yes, I often work upstairs,' said Luke. 'If Raphael and Jemma aren't in, I run the shop.'

'Jolly good, jolly good.' He transferred his hand to Em. 'And Em is short for . . . Emma?'

'It's Emily, actually,' said Em. 'But no one calls me that.' Jemma couldn't believe she had admitted it. She knew how much Em hated her name.

'That's a pity,' said Lennox, shaking his head. 'Emily is a very pretty name, and, of course, a distinguished one. Emily Brontë, Emily Dickinson…' His gaze fell on Maddy, who, to Jemma's surprise, was blushing furiously and studying the table. 'There's no need to be shy,' he said. 'I won't bite.' Was it Jemma's imagination, or had his eyes flicked towards Luke for a moment?

Maddy giggled, which Jemma put down to nerves.

'I remember you, Maddy,' Lennox continued. 'Did you work for Brian? I'm sure we met on one of my flying visits to the UK.'

If anything, Maddy's blush deepened. 'Yes, we did,' she got out.

'I thought so.' Introductions complete, he turned his attention back to Jemma. 'I'm terribly sorry if I startled you, but Raphael gave me a key. As I couldn't see anyone in the bookshop, I decided that letting myself in was the best option. Then I heard voices downstairs, and came to find you.'

'That's interesting,' said Jemma. 'We didn't hear you until that door opened.'

'I hope I didn't make you jump,' said Lennox, but there was a gleam in his eye.

I'd love to know how you got in here without making any noise, thought Jemma. *Have you enchanted the bookshop?* Then she noticed that his eye had fallen on Folio.

'I hope that cat isn't in the bookshop during opening hours,' he said, and the scrunching-up of his nose was visible for all to see.

'Yes, he is,' said Jemma. 'The customers love him, and people come to the bookshop just to see Folio. He's famous, you know.'

'Is he,' said Lennox, continuing to regard Folio with distaste.

Folio regarded the newcomer through narrowed eyes and, lifting a leg in the air, began to lick his stomach. Jemma was principally glad that he hadn't chosen his bottom.

'Ugh.' Lennox turned away. 'Raphael made me aware that he still had a cat, but he never mentioned that it was allowed free rein in the shop. I dread to think what public health would make of it. Especially as you have a café.'

'Folio is a very clean cat,' said Em. 'Anyway, he doesn't usually come near the café. It's too busy for him.'

'Small mercies,' said Lennox. 'Anyway, I won't keep you long. I only came to introduce myself as your new Keeper and to take a look at the place. We'll begin in earnest tomorrow; I have a speaking engagement tonight.'

Of course you do. 'Have you come far?' she said.

'Oh no.' He gave her an indulgent smile. 'A dear friend of mine happens to be in France this year, so she offered me her little pied-à-terre near St James's. So handy for Fortnum's. Anyway, enough of that. Why don't you give me a quick tour?' He started to take his coat off, then thought better of it. 'Is the shop always this cold?'

For the first time since his arrival, Jemma considered

her surroundings. The shop was definitely a few degrees cooler than normal. 'It's usually warmer than this,' she admitted. 'I think it's getting used to you.' She was quite proud of her tact.

'Temperamental, is it?' He laughed. 'Good old Raphael, always so soft-hearted. I imagine you've been putting up with this shop's tricks for years. I'm afraid I don't have time for that.' He raised his right hand and seemed to grip an invisible dial, then turned it ninety degrees clockwise. Immediately, the shop's temperature climbed until it was cosy. 'That's better.' He removed his coat and draped it over an armchair. 'Let's start in here.'

He strolled round the shelves with Jemma, peering at the books and every so often firing a question at her. Some were easy to deal with, such as which genres sold best, how much money the shop had made the previous month, and what proportion of those profits derived from the café. Others, such as profit per shelving unit, the average cost of each book purchased, and the long-term stock acquisition plan, she tried to fend off with statements such as 'I'll put a report together for you', or 'I'll consult the database'.

'You manage the Friendly Bookshop, too.' It was a statement, not a question.

'Yes, I do,' said Jemma. 'Raphael acquired it last autumn and asked me to run it. After studying the bookshops in the area, I have transformed it from an antiquarian bookshop specialising in non-fiction to a general bookshop stocking good quality and collectible books—'

'Yes, yes.' He waved a hand impatiently. 'And you have

been an Assistant Keeper since…'

'Last autumn,' said Jemma. 'I was acting in the role first.'

'So three or four months.' He inspected her in a way that made her want to wriggle. 'Still in your probationary period.'

'I have been formally appointed to the role—'

'Which comes with a six-month probation.' This smile was much less charming than his previous ones. 'No need to look embarrassed, Jemma, I'm not trying to catch you out. As you've seen, though, I am not as soft-hearted as Raphael. I dare say he has painted me as a jet-setting academic and jack of all trades.' His smile was infused with satisfaction. 'To a degree, he is right. However, the bedrock of my achievements has been the support of a reliable, efficient team.'

He gazed around the cavernous lower floor. 'Raphael, I have no doubt, would be content to muddle along with a shop in disarray, overrun by cats and doing as it pleases. I, however, am less tolerant. As I have more important things to do than mind a secondhand bookshop, I shall be fulfilling engagements, and of course my Keeper duties, all of which is best done in the field. When I do materialise in the bookshop' – Jemma recalled their shock when the oak door had opened – 'everything will run smoothly, and any information should be at your fingertips.' He surveyed them, and somehow he seemed taller. 'I trust I make myself clear.'

'Yes, Lennox,' they chorused, like schoolchildren caught out by their teacher in a minor misdemeanour.

'Oh yes, one more thing. I would prefer you to address me as Dr Nash, particularly in front of the customers. I have earned my title, and I expect it to be used.' He smiled again, but only Maddy smiled back. 'There, Maddy understands. I must go now, but I expect you all in bright and early tomorrow. As you closed early today, you had better open at eight thirty to make up for it. Goodnight.' He scooped up his coat and strode away. 'Remove that cat from the shop, please,' he called over his shoulder. 'I don't wish to see it tomorrow.'

The oak door banged shut, and his footsteps ascended the stairs. A few seconds later, they heard the jangle of the bell.

'I didn't know *he* would be our new boss,' said Maddy, brightly. 'That's lucky, isn't it?'

***

On the way home, Jemma took a detour by way of Snacking Cross Road, where she picked up a twelve-inch pepperoni pizza. If Carl wasn't there to share it with her, she had every intention of finishing it solo. She let herself into the shop, took her laptop from under the counter, and went up to the flat. Given the reports Lennox Nash had asked for, it would be a long evening.

'There you are!' Carl bounced up from the sofa. 'Did you get my text?'

Jemma shook her head. She hadn't checked her phone since mid-afternoon, but she didn't remember it buzzing.

'I texted to ask you to meet me at the pub, but you didn't reply, so I came here. We could go out to eat.' He saw the pizza box. 'Bad day?' His face fell. 'Sorry. I feel bad now.'

'Why?' Jemma took him in. 'Oh. It's good news, then.'

'It's amazing news.' His expression was guarded. 'Well, for me.'

Jemma put the pizza box on the coffee table and sat on the sofa. 'Tell me.'

'I've got a backer to take *A New Leaf* on tour. And they liked my pitch for the new play. Subject to seeing the full manuscript, they'll try it in rehearsal and stage it in a small London theatre when we come back.'

'When you come back?'

'Yes.' Carl sat on the sofa beside her and took her hand. 'I'm the director and the playwright. They want me to go too.'

Chapter 8

Jemma wondered, briefly, what else in her world could crash down in one day. 'How long will the tour be?' she asked. Her mouth was dry.

'We're going up one side of the country and down the other,' said Carl.

'What, it's arranged already?'

'Yes. Basically, they decided to pull the play they'd scheduled. Production difficulties. *A New Leaf* is the replacement. That's why it's been such a rush.'

'So how long will you be away? Do you need to be there for all of it?'

Carl shrugged. 'Certainly at the beginning. Later, maybe not. But Michael – that's the promoter – wants me to do interviews and appearances. Meet the playwright, maybe some workshops. He thinks that will get bums on seats, as he put it.' His smile wavered. 'I'm not sure, but he's the boss and it's good pay. Hopefully, once it's over, I can hole up here and concentrate on writing for a change.'

Jemma imagined Carl in a whirlwind of activity, doing

interviews, taking charge of rehearsals, and making friends, while she was stuck shuttling between two bookshops under the watchful eye of Lennox Nash. 'You still haven't said how long you'll be gone.' Her tone was sharper than she had meant.

Carl gave her a hurt look. 'Three or four months, initially. I'm sure I'll be able to return for days off sometimes, and like I said, maybe they won't need me so much later. But we have to find some new cast members. Three of Rumpus are up for this, but two don't want to leave London for so long. So there'll be auditions, followed by intensive rehearsals, and then we go. First stop, Dover.'

All Jemma could think was that Carl didn't seem to mind being away from London for months at a time. Away from his family, and her.

Carl reached over and put an arm round her. 'I'm sorry, Jemma. I knew you wouldn't be as happy as I am, but it's a once-in-a-lifetime opportunity. I mean, this time last year I was working in a coffee shop and auditioning for parts, and now I'm taking my play on tour. I'm taking *my play* on tour. I never thought it would happen.'

'I understand,' said Jemma, and she did. *This had to happen now. My whole life's falling apart, and there's nothing I can do.* She sighed. 'We'd better get this pizza eaten before it goes cold. I know you like it cold, but I don't. Do you want a Diet Coke?' She got up and went to the kitchen area.

'Wait, Jemma, I'll get it,' Carl said, as Jemma opened the fridge and saw the bottle of champagne in the door. She closed it, put her hand on the fridge, and gritted her teeth.

He was beside her in a moment, and took her in his arms. 'I'm sorry, Jemma. I didn't realise it would hit you so hard.'

'I'm fine,' murmured Jemma. 'I'll be fine. It's just been a hard day. Saying goodbye to Raphael and – and everything.'

'Oh yeah, the new Keeper.' He waited, but Jemma said nothing. 'Jemma, talk to me. What happened today?'

'He's the guy I did the interviews with in Berkshire. We didn't get on then, and we don't now. He thinks I don't know what I'm doing.'

'That's rubbish, for a start.'

'He doesn't want Folio in the bookshop.'

'What?' Carl stared at her. 'The customers will freak out. Did Folio do something?'

'No, he just doesn't like cats. And he controlled the shop. He turned the temperature up with his hand and the shop had to obey. The weirdest thing is that Maddy thinks he's great.'

'I take it the others don't,' said Carl. 'Shall we have a drink anyway? It's a shame to waste the champagne.' He looked rather embarrassed. 'I've never bought a bottle of champagne before. I thought they might ask me for ID at the checkout.'

Jemma managed a smile. 'I shouldn't, I've got work to do. Lennox – Dr Nash – wants information, and I'll have to dig for it.' She glanced at the laptop bag which she had left in the doorway. 'He wants both shops open at eight thirty tomorrow morning.'

'Throwing his weight around, huh.' Carl opened the fridge and took out the champagne. 'He's probably being extra strict because he's new. Like when a new teacher joins the school and they come down hard on everyone. Hopefully he'll settle.' He removed the foil and inspected the cork. 'You do whatever you need to, and I'll bring you a drink.'

'Thanks.' Jemma fetched the laptop, took a notepad from her bag, and settled into a corner of the sofa. She stretched her wrists out to type, and remembered. 'I won't be a moment.' She went through to the bedroom and opened the jewellery box on the chest of drawers. Inside was a small black box. She removed the lid and studied the slim silver bracelet Raphael had given her for Christmas. Two stones – one deep yellow, one purple – shone up at her, one on either side. She attempted to put the bracelet on, but the clasp kept slipping. She went into the sitting room and held out her left wrist. 'Can you help me with this?'

Carl set down the bottle. 'Why are you putting that on? We aren't going anywhere. Are we?'

'It was something Raphael said. I don't know if it will help, but maybe it's worth a try.' *Anything is worth a try right now.*

***

Jemma woke the next morning with a heavy weight on her calves. She reached down and stroked Luna. 'When did you arrive?' she murmured. Then she opened her eyes and saw the note propped against her bedside lamp. She switched the lamp on, as it was still dark, and read:

Tried to wake you but you were sound asleep. Hope today goes better. Meeting with Michael and Janina first thing to discuss spec for new actors and do a couple of interviews. Would have said last night but it didn't feel right. Stay strong. I'll text. Love you X

Jemma's alarm shrilled. She pulled her feet from underneath Luna, who squeaked in protest, and padded wearily to the bathroom to face the day.

By a quarter past eight the sign on the door of the Friendly Bookshop said *Open*, but as expected, there were no customers. *At least the shop's nice and tidy*, thought Jemma. *He can't find fault with that.*

Maddy arrived at twenty past eight wearing a long black dress with a lace collar and low-heeled boots, her hair pulled back in a tight plait. She could have been a Victorian schoolmarm. 'He isn't here yet?' She sounded disappointed.

'He'll probably go to Burns Books first,' said Jemma. 'I'd better head over with these reports. Hopefully I won't be long.' She gulped the rest of her tea, put the folder of documents into her bag, and opened the door.

On the doorstep sat Folio, but he was not the sleek, plump cat of the day before. He seemed to have shrunk, and his ginger fur was matted into knots. He gazed up at her, his eyes still dark, and gave a piteous little meow.

'Folio!' She scooped him up and cuddled him. He was much lighter than usual. 'Haven't you had breakfast? Come with me.' She took him into the back room, set him down carefully, and found a tin of food. 'I'm sorry it isn't salmon,' she said as she forked it onto a plate. 'I'll fetch some tins when I go over to Burns Books. You stay here today.' She put the plate on the floor and Folio looked at it as if he wasn't sure what to do.

'Are you thirsty? Wait a minute.' She filled a bowl at the tap. Folio lapped at it a couple of times, then sat down.

Maddy came to see. 'You can't let Dr Nash see him in the bookshop,' she said. 'There'll be trouble.'

'Yes, I know,' said Jemma. 'But he needs care. Look at him.' She stroked the rough coat, and bit her lip as she remembered how smooth and glossy he had been. 'I'm fetching Luna.'

'You'll be late,' said Maddy, but Jemma was already on her way.

Luna was still curled on her bed, fast asleep. 'Luna!' called Jemma. She heard a little meow behind her and Folio leapt onto the bed.

One sleepy green eye opened, then the other. Luna stretched out a long black foreleg and pulled Folio down beside her. Out came her little pink tongue, and she began to lick the top of his head.

And at last, Folio purred.

***

'Bright and early, eh,' said Jemma at a quarter to eleven.

So far, their customers had included one man who had asked if he could use the toilet, then left without so much as glancing at the shelves, one harassed woman towing a toddler dressed in football kit, who had bought a takeaway coffee and departed, and an elderly gentleman who was comfortably settled in an armchair reading a Raymond Chandler novel. Jemma suspected he wasn't planning to pay for it when he had finished.

'Do as I say, not as I do,' Luke replied, and scowled out of the window.

'At least the bookshop is behaving,' said Jemma. On her way to Burns Books she had imagined a scene of devastation. The shop had been perfectly tidy when they locked up, but it could easily have undone that overnight.

Luke's lip curled. 'It probably doesn't dare do anything else. He's got the shop under his thumb.' He glared around him as if he wanted the shop to start shooting books onto the floor. 'How's Maddy this morning?' He said the words casually, but the look he gave Jemma was a mixture of anger and concern.

Luke doesn't know... Jemma shrugged. 'Wearing a dress with a lace collar. Disapproving of Folio. Disappointed Dr Nash hasn't appeared yet.'

Luke snorted. 'That figures. She said she was busy last night and went home.' His nose wrinkled. 'Guess who's on his way.'

Perhaps half a minute later, the bell jangled and Lennox Nash strode in, wearing a tweed suit this time, with a knitted maroon tie and brogues. 'Hello, hello,' he said. Then he stopped. 'Where are the customers?'

Luke shrugged. 'Not here, obviously.'

'I can see that. Not very good, is it? Saturday ought to be a peak sales day.'

Jemma dived into her bag. 'I've printed those reports,

Dr Nash.'

'Ah, yes.' He peeped inside the folder and handed it back to her. 'I haven't time to peruse them now, I'm afraid. Just calling in before I catch my train. Off to the country, as you see.' He indicated the tweed suit. 'Where were we? Oh yes, this is a poor show. Maybe you could pop some boxes of books outside. Or even better, one of you could go out with a sandwich board. Yes, get a sandwich board ordered. Pass me that notepad.' He took a fountain pen from an inner pocket, uncapped it, and wrote in neat capitals *COME TO BURNS BOOKS AND BE ENTRANCED*. 'That and the address should do it.'

Jemma, stunned, opened her mouth to reply, but her phone rang. She fished it out of her bag and checked the display: *Jasper Bantam*. 'Hello, Jasper.'

'Good morning, Jemma,' said Jasper. 'I hope this isn't a bad time. I wondered if you could pop over.'

'No, it's fine,' said Jemma, trying not to grin. 'What can I do for you?'

'We've got a – well, an interesting book at the library. Nothing like last time,' he added hastily. 'No atmospheric changes or vibrations, but it seems to be attracting other books.'

'How do you mean? Like a magnet?'

'That's exactly it: a magnet.' She could hear the smile in his voice. 'I knew you'd be able to help.'

'I can try. What grade of emergency would you say it is?'

'Low-level, I think, if you can sort it quickly. Then we could go for coffee. Or lunch, if it takes longer than we thought.'

'I'll get there as soon as I can,' said Jemma. 'See you soon, Jasper. Bye.' She ended the call, and looked up to see Luke and Lennox watching her.

'Can I come too?' said Luke.

'A knowledge emergency? Whereabouts?' asked Lennox.

'At the London Library,' said Jemma, reaching for the kitbag and putting it on the counter. 'I shouldn't be long.'

Lennox picked it up. 'I'll take that. The London Library is a hop, skip and a jump from my place, and I need to pop back for my bag.' He put the kitbag over his shoulder, where it sat incongruously against his tweed suit. 'Jasper who?'

'Jasper Bantam,' said Jemma. 'And he rang *me*, because—'

'Don't remember him; must be new. Good opportunity to size him up. I won't have time to come back, so I'll see you on Monday. Bright and early.' He made for the door, then turned. 'Don't forget: sandwich board.' And with that, he was gone.

Jemma picked up the notepad he had written on, flung it across the shop, and burst into tears. 'Sorry,' she choked out, and fled to the staff toilet.

After a couple of minutes, Luke knocked quietly on the door. 'Jemma? Jemma, are you all right? I'm sorry you're upset.' But as hot tears trickled down Jemma's cheeks, she knew very well that she was not upset, but furious.

Chapter 9

The grandfather clock in the corner struck twelve. 'Time for lunch,' said Maddy. She closed the book catalogue she was reading and put it away. 'Are you sure Dr Nash won't be coming back today?'

'Quite sure,' said Jemma. 'He's going somewhere for the weekend. He's already given us our orders.' Secretly, she hoped the mysterious book at the London Library had got the better of Lennox Nash. However, having seen the effect he had had on Burns Books, she wasn't optimistic. Besides, Jasper would have phoned her if anything were amiss.

'I expect he'll visit us on Monday,' said Maddy, brightening.

'I'm afraid Dr Nash's absence means that you and Luke will have to take your lunches separately today,' said Jemma. 'I'll eat mine here, then cover for Luke when you return.'

'That's fine,' said Maddy, with a toss of her head. She unhooked her parka and put it on. It looked incongruous with her long black dress. 'Do we have any poetry books?'

'A few. Our customers don't often buy them. Most of them are in the window at the moment for Valentine's Day.'

Maddy sniffed.

'Do you want anything in particular?'

Maddy put her hands in her pockets. 'I've never read any Emily Dickinson.'

'Oh.' Jemma went to the poetry section. 'Sorry, no. I bet another bookshop will stock her poems, though. You could try Burns Books. In fact, if you go there first, you can tell Luke that I'll cover his lunch.'

'I'm sure Luke can work that out for himself,' said Maddy, and left.

The atmosphere of the bookshop lightened once the door closed behind Maddy. *What's got into her?* thought Jemma. *Is it Lennox Nash?* She remembered when Maddy had been under a spell before, and her erratic, hostile behaviour. This wasn't anything like as bad, but still troubling. And now there was a new emergency at the London Library... 'I wish I knew what to do,' Jemma said aloud. She looked around guiltily, then realised it didn't matter. The shop was empty, as it had been almost all morning. That felt like a sort of spell, too, as if the shop had somehow become cut off from the rest of Charing Cross Road.

Raphael would know what to do. Before she knew it, Jemma had her phone in her hand and her contact list open. *Should I? He might still be travelling.*

If he's travelling, he won't be able to answer his phone

anyway. Jemma punched the Call button, and waited for a connection.

After a few seconds, nothing had happened. No dial tone, no engaged tone, no recorded message. 'Odd,' she said, and tried again. Nothing.

She thought of ringing Carl, but he was probably in a meeting. She scrolled up to *Burns Books*, and dialled. No connection, no signal, and no internet connection either.

'Oh, for heaven's sake!' Yet the phone had been fine earlier, when she'd taken Jasper's call at Burns Books. She gazed at the phone, a horrible suspicion growing in her mind. *Has Lennox done something to it?*

She hurried to the door and turned the sign to *Closed*, then went up to her own flat. Luna ran into the vestibule as she shut the door, and Folio peeped out behind her. 'Sorry, emergency,' she told them, and called again. Still no.

'Aaargh!' She paced up and down the living room, then caught sight of her laptop, which she had left on the coffee table the evening before. 'I wonder…' She opened the lid, found the right app, and typed in Raphael's number from her phone. She pressed *Call*, and a message flashed up: *Calling...* 'Thank goodness,' she whispered.

The cats jumped on the sofa beside her and settled, an untidy yin and yang symbol. Folio's coat was still rough, but much less matted. She stroked them both while she waited.

After twenty seconds, the message changed to *Connecting*. A black square appeared, which resolved itself into Raphael, wearing a pale-blue shirt and a cream suit jacket. She wasn't sure she liked this new, smart Raphael.

He was sitting in a restaurant and a glass of red wine was visible to his left. 'Er, hello, Jemma,' he said.

'Hi, Raphael,' said Jemma. 'Sorry to ring so soon.'

'Is the bookshop still standing?'

'Er, yes, it is, but—'

'Did Lennox turn up last night?'

'Yes, he did, and he doesn't like Folio. Folio is really upset; he's got smaller and his fur is a mess.' She felt guilty for beginning with Folio, but she judged that if anything would bring Raphael back, it would be the cat he had owned for hundreds of years.

'I had a feeling Folio wouldn't be happy,' said Raphael. 'Hopefully he'll get used to things.'

'He's here, if you want to see him.'

'I'm not sure that's a good idea,' said Raphael. 'It'll upset him.'

Luna lifted her head, so that she was just in shot, and meowed.

'Oh good, there's Luna. Is she helping? I'm sure she is.'

Luna laid her head on her paws in disgust. 'Still off colour, maybe,' said Raphael. 'Have you taken her to the vet yet?'

'I haven't had time,' Jemma snapped. 'I've been busy tidying, sorting and being insulted by your replacement. Who, by the way, breezed in for five minutes this morning, told us we were doing a bad job, then left for a weekend in the country. Oh yes, and when Jasper Bantam rang about a knowledge emergency at the London Library he took it upon himself to go, even though Jasper rang me.'

'Oh dear.' Raphael glanced to the side. 'It's Jemma,' he

murmured, followed by some rapid Italian. He faced her again. 'Was it a serious emergency?'

'Jasper didn't think so, but that isn't the point. He asked *me* to go.'

'Maybe Lennox thought he was doing you a favour,' said Raphael.

'Oh yes, and we're not allowed to call him Lennox. Dr Nash to us.'

'Well, that is his title.'

'In that case, maybe I'll insist that he calls me Ms James.'

Raphael laughed. 'Jemma, aren't you taking this a little too seriously?'

'You weren't there!' cried Jemma, and both the cats looked up. 'He sneaked into the shop, told us off for closing early, banned Folio from the shop during opening hours, made a point of reminding me that I'm still on probation, demanded reports which he hasn't even read, and ordered us to open early today for no reason. He's a complete dictator. The only person who likes him is Maddy, and that's weird too.'

Raphael said nothing for a moment, then sipped from his glass of wine. 'Tell me about this knowledge emergency. Jasper rang you, you say.'

'Yes. Jasper said it seemed minor, but a book was attracting other books. I don't know any more, because I didn't get to go and see.'

'I'd think nothing of it if it wasn't the London Library,' said Raphael. 'As it is… Jemma, will you ask Lennox about it on Monday? You could say you'll do the paperwork for him. He'll like that; he isn't keen on paperwork.'

'OK,' said Jemma, although she was tempted to tell Raphael to ask Lennox himself. 'There's something else. He controlled the bookshop. It was cold, and he made it get warmer.'

'Oh yes,' said Raphael. 'That's one of his party tricks.'

'But the bookshop didn't want to! He forced it!'

'He's in charge,' said Raphael. 'It isn't what I'd do, but it would be a dull world if we were all the same. Our lunch is approaching; I must go. Wait – are you wearing your bracelet?'

Jemma held up her wrist. 'You still haven't told me what it does.'

'All in good time,' said Raphael. Giulia murmured something in Italian, and he laughed. 'Goodbye, Jemma.' Instantly, he was replaced by a black rectangle.

Jemma closed the app, shut the laptop, and took it downstairs. *At least this works, even if my phone doesn't.* She fetched her sandwich and looked for a book to read while she waited for Maddy's return, since she didn't expect a flood of customers any time soon. But nothing on the shelves appealed; everything was too heavy, too light, too dense, or too dull.

She put her sandwich on the counter and went to switch on the kettle. As it rumbled to life she thought of Raphael, sitting in an Italian restaurant drinking wine and eating a proper lunch with Giulia, while she made do with a ham-salad sandwich and an empty shop. Her eyes prickled and she blinked hard. *Don't be ridiculous, Jemma. You've already had one crying fit today. Don't start another.* She had a thought, checked the diary app on her phone, then laughed. Her period was due in the next few days. 'Stupid hormones,' she murmured, and eyed the bracelet on her left wrist. 'What *does* it do?'

The kettle pinged and she made tea, leaving the teabag in for an extra minute. *At least I don't have to deal with Lennox Nash again till Monday*, she thought. *Carl and I can celebrate properly tonight. He deserves it.* She checked her phone, but there were no new texts or notifications from Carl or anyone else. *Just as I thought.* She pushed the teabag against the side of the mug, squeezing the life out of it, then flicked it at the bin and scored a direct hit. Somehow, that made her feel better.

Chapter 10

Maddy returned from lunch with a tight, smug expression. Jemma got up from her chair. 'I'll go to Burns Books and cover for Luke. I may be a while; I need to discuss stock with Em.'

Maddy's eyes narrowed. 'I thought you'd already done that. Weren't you doing a report the other day?'

'Yes, but when I was putting together those extra reports for – for Dr Nash, I saw a couple of other things to pick up.'

The hard, accusing lines of Maddy's expression smoothed themselves out. 'Oh, well if it's for the business, I can certainly look after things here.'

'I know you can,' said Jemma. She felt bad for fibbing to Maddy, but the sight of her in that long black dress was getting on Jemma's nerves. 'I can ask about that poetry book if you like, or bring you something from the café.'

Maddy's face lit up. 'Yes please to the book… Don't worry about food; I had a bacon roll for lunch. Proper hot, crispy bacon.' A smile played over her lips, and Jemma could have sworn that she was actually salivating.

'I thought you were practically vegan.'

'I try to eat healthily,' said Maddy, 'but sometimes I crave well-done meat. A little of what you fancy.'

'Mmm. I'll be off, then.' Jemma put a notepad and pen into her bag to lend credence to her story and left Maddy standing at the counter, still dreaming of bacon.

As she walked to Burns Books, she puzzled. What could have made Maddy eat a bacon sandwich for the first time since she had known her? Luke stayed away from animal products, even drinking a vegan blood substitute he bought on the internet, though occasionally he succumbed to the lure of raw meat. Crispy bacon, however, was something else. *At least I don't have to worry about love bites.* She would never have thought she would regret the change.

Burns Books, like the Friendly Bookshop, was uncharacteristically quiet for a Saturday. Luke was leaning on the counter, reading, but as soon as he saw Jemma, he slammed the book shut and shoved it under the counter. Jemma suspected it was a relationship manual. 'Hi, Jemma. Come to put in the order for that sandwich board?' His grin was forced, mirthless.

'You have to be kidding. There's no way I'm parading up and down Charing Cross Road wearing a sandwich board, and I don't expect any of you to do it either. I'm here to take over the till so you can get some lunch.'

Luke shrugged. 'Already had mine. It hasn't exactly been buzzing today, so you can head back.'

Jemma scrutinised Luke. His shoulders drooped more

than usual, and there was an awkwardness to his movements. 'Hopefully things will improve,' she said. 'I'll just pop downstairs and see Em. With everything else going on, we've barely spoken this week.'

Downstairs, a couple of customers were inspecting the shelves. They weren't holding any books, though. Jemma dreaded to think what their takings would be at the end of the day. Em, meanwhile, was standing at the café counter, folding a napkin into the shape of a swan. 'Hi,' she said, finishing the swan and setting it on the counter, where it fell over. 'What can I do for you?'

'Have you got time for a drink?'

The corner of Em's mouth turned up. 'What do you think?'

She made cappuccinos and brought them to a small table by the counter. 'How's things at the Friendly Bookshop?'

'Everything's awful,' said Jemma. 'And Carl is taking his play on tour.'

'On tour?' Em stared at her. 'When? Where?'

'As soon as possible, and around the UK.' Jemma sipped her cappuccino and put the cup down. Now she had actually said the words, it sounded ridiculous.

'When did you find this out?'

'Yesterday evening. He'd said there was a possibility of something big, and he'd been in lots of meetings for a couple of days, but it was out of the blue.'

'That isn't good.' Em drank some coffee.

'Well no, it's not ideal, but it's only for a few months. He may be able to get some days off.'

'Mm. He still lives at his mum's, doesn't he?'

'He spends lots of time at my place.' Jemma heard the defensive note in her voice. They had spent more time lately gazing at laptops than each other: Carl attempting to make headway on his second play while she did paperwork. She couldn't remember the last time they had gone out properly together. 'Anyway, it's winter. It's too cold to do much.'

Em studied her over the rim of her cup. 'You're not worried, then.'

'Worried? Me?' Jemma's cup clacked on the saucer. 'No, I'm not worried. Carl will be too busy to do much except work.'

Em appeared to be wondering what to say next. 'I'm sure you're right,' she said, eventually.

'Yes,' said Jemma, and realised she had nothing else to say. She got up and walked to the poetry shelves. Sure enough, *Selected Poems of Emily Dickinson* was sitting on the top row. 'I'm borrowing this.'

Em's eyebrows shot up. 'You're reading Emily Dickinson?'

'Maddy asked me to look.'

Em made a dismissive noise. 'Oh, Maddy. She's got it bad.'

'You shouldn't be rude about other staff members,' said Jemma, putting aside her own feelings towards Maddy.

'Whatever,' said Em, and took her cup back to the counter.

'I'll see myself out,' said Jemma, though no one was listening. More than ever, she resolved that she and Carl would have a night out together, whether he wanted one or not.

She spent the rest of the afternoon serving a meagre sprinkling of customers while Maddy devoured poetry, leaning against *General Fiction T-Z*. Jemma could see her lips moving, and remembered what Em had said. Was this just a crush, or something more sinister?

She told Maddy to go at four o'clock. Maddy made no protest, tucking the book into her bag and walking to the door with a soppy smile on her face. 'Bye, Jemma,' she called. 'See you on Monday.' Her smile brightened, presumably because she had remembered she might see Lennox on Monday. *Maybe she's planning to recite Emily Dickinson at him*, thought Jemma. She managed to hold in her laughter until the door closed.

At five o'clock her phone buzzed repeatedly. She checked it and found various notifications, messages, and missed calls. Carl had phoned twice, leaving a message the second time. 'Hi Jemma, just checking in. It's going really well. Don't start cooking or whatever; I'm going for a drink with Michael and Janina when we finish. See you later, bye.'

Jemma's thumbs flew over the keyboard. *What time will you be back? I've booked a table.* She pressed *Send*. *Well, I will have in a couple of minutes.* She called the local Greek restaurant. As she got through her phone buzzed, but she didn't look till she had secured a table for two at eight o'clock. If they had had one earlier, she would have grabbed it.

She read Carl's message: *Where? I fancied a quiet night*

in.

She replied: *Acropolis at 8. Meze or stifado?*

She had to wait a few minutes for his next response. *OK. See you later.*

She had ended up leaving alone for the restaurant at ten to eight. *He had better turn up*, she thought as she hurried down the road, wobbling slightly on the heels she hadn't worn since last year. At least Nic, the owner, was pleased to see her. She sat nursing a glass of red wine till quarter past eight, when Carl finally came through the door dressed in his smartest shirt. She beamed at him, then remembered that he had probably been wearing it all day, as he'd left before she woke up.

'You made it,' she said, pushing a menu towards him.

'Yeah.' He sank into his seat with a huff of breath. 'I swear the tube gets worse, not better. Still, not for much longer.'

Jemma nearly spat out her wine. 'Nice to see you too,' she remarked, when she had safely swallowed it.

Annoyance flashed across his face. 'Don't be like that, Jemma. It isn't personal. It's a rotten journey, and you know it.'

'Sorry,' she said, not feeling it. 'How did it go?'

'Busy. Janina called a few agents and we managed to see some actors this afternoon. We found a couple who'll suit, which is good because it saves time on auditions, but we need to crack on with rehearsals. And Michael wants to do that in Dover.'

Jemma stared at him. 'You aren't serious.'

'Yep,' said Carl. 'It makes sense. We've got three

weeks' run and Janina knows people at the theatre. She reckons we can rehearse there in the mornings.'

Janina this, Janina that. Jemma hoped Janina was old, unfashionable, and terrifying. 'So you'll be leaving sooner than we thought,' she said.

Carl put his hand on hers. 'I'm sorry, Jemma. I know this has happened really quickly.'

I'm not going to cry in the middle of a Greek restaurant. Jemma took a gulp of wine and set the glass on the table, then rolled the stem between her fingers and watched the glass spin. 'It's fine.'

***

Late on Sunday afternoon, she watched Carl throw socks into his sports bag. 'I wish you didn't have to go.'

'So do I.' He turned to her and she saw various emotions working in his face: excitement, sadness, and possibly a little impatience. 'It isn't for ever, Jemma; it's only a few months. I'm in and out here, anyway.'

It was true. While Carl kept underpants, socks, and a few clothes at Jemma's flat, most of his stuff was still at his mum's. He had never moved in as such, just begun to spend more evenings a week at her place. But it still felt as if he was moving out.

'Maybe you could come and see me, if we're somewhere nice,' he said, checking the drawer of the bedside table. 'You could come on a Sunday, spend the day with me on Monday and see the play, and travel back on Tuesday.'

'Couldn't I come on Friday and stay for the weekend?'

Carl screwed his mouth up. 'We do a matinee on

Saturday, so I'd be in the theatre practically all day.' He began to zip up his bag, then stopped. 'I'll check the bathroom.'

Jemma followed him. 'It's just that I don't know when I'll be able to take leave. I doubt my new boss is particularly considerate about personal stuff.' Carl took his toothbrush out of the mug. 'Do you have to take that? You must have a toothbrush at your mum's.'

He sighed and put it back. 'Yeah, I suppose. I can always buy another.'

Jemma wanted to shake him, to cry out, 'Don't you understand that I'm scared I'll never see you again?' But he was already walking into the bedroom, zipping his bag, scanning the room for anything he might have missed.

'If you came here instead, we could plan dates,' said Jemma. 'Go to the movies, get tickets for a play—'

Carl laughed. 'That sounds like a busman's holiday. It's a nice idea, though.' He leaned down and kissed her briefly on the mouth. 'I'll FaceTime you, yeah? Give the cats a stroke from me.' For a moment, he looked disappointed. 'I thought they'd see me off.'

'I think they're busy,' said Jemma. In fact, Luna had meowed to be let out when Jemma and Carl had got back from the restaurant, and Folio had followed like her shadow.

'Catching mice, I expect,' Carl said carelessly. He hefted his bag and walked to the door. 'You don't have to come downstairs with me. I hate goodbyes.'

'I'll lock up, anyway,' said Jemma, and trailed after him to the main door. They hugged, hampered by Carl's sports bag, and he strode away. He looked round once, and raised a hand in farewell. Then his pace quickened.

She heard a little meow at her feet and saw Luna's green eyes, luminous in the dusk. 'So you're back,' she said. 'Is Folio there?'

Another meow came from a dark corner and Folio stepped forward.

'Come along, you two, time for your dinner.' She opened tins and refilled the biscuit bowl, which was empty.

Folio nibbled at his tinned food, but Luna gobbled hers up, then started on her biscuits. 'You'll get a tummy ache,' said Jemma, but she kept eating.

Jemma considered what to cook for herself, but she didn't feel hungry in the slightest. Instead she sat on the sofa, imagining Carl sitting on the tube, nodding to the music in his headphones and anticipating his big adventure. The cats arranged themselves on her lap, and once they had settled Jemma searched her memory for the good times she had shared with Carl. But the pictures in her mind seemed distant and faded: as if they had happened long ago, to someone else entirely.

Chapter 11

Jemma woke surprisingly refreshed, but covered in cats: Luna was balanced on her hip, Folio sprawled across her knees. Her left forefinger was also sandwiched between the pages of *I Capture The Castle*, though the reading lamp was switched off. *How did I do that?* Then she realised Carl wasn't there. Still, he hadn't been there much during the last week. *I'll have to get used to it.* She yawned, stretched, and saw the silver bracelet on her wrist. *I must find out what it does. And there are other things to find out, too.*

Forty-five minutes later, she was showered, dressed, breakfasted, and heading down to the bookshop, Luna and Folio slinking behind her. *He'd better not say anything about the cats being in the Friendly Bookshop*, she thought. *It's my bookshop, not his. Not that Burns Books is his either, although you wouldn't think it from the way he behaves.*

She was just opening up when she saw Maddy coming along the road, wearing another long black dress. She had plaited her hair again, but this time, pinned it in a circle on top of her head. The hairstyle made her seem older and more severe, but emphasised her long, graceful neck. *Luke would probably love it*, thought Jemma. *If he gets to see it.* She had a distinct feeling that Maddy's new hairstyle was not for Luke's benefit.

'Good morning, Maddy, how was your weekend?'

'Very nice, thank you,' said Maddy. 'I read *Little Women*.'

'Really? I wouldn't have thought that was your sort of thing.'

Maddy frowned. 'Why wouldn't it be my sort of thing?' She walked into the shop, hung up her parka, and touched her plaits self-consciously.

'It's a bit different from *Dracula*, isn't it?'

Maddy's nose wrinkled. 'A change is as good as a rest, they say. I'll put the kettle on.' She went through to the back room. Something felt familiar, but Jemma couldn't put her finger on it. She only figured it out when Maddy returned with two mugs of tea. Lennox Nash's nose had wrinkled in a similar way when he had looked at Luke.

'Did you enjoy the poetry book?' she asked, for something to say.

An odd, watchful expression came over Maddy's face, as if she had a secret she couldn't tell. 'I did, yes.' She put her mug down and went to the fiction shelves, scanning them as she walked slowly along the aisle.

Jemma moved slightly to get a better view. As she had expected, Maddy stopped at B. *I must get to the bottom of this.*

After a moment, Maddy said, 'I'll check the stockroom.' Jemma had a feeling that if she had been in the way, Maddy might well have pushed past her in her quest. However, she happened to know that they currently had no copies of *Wuthering Heights*.

Two minutes later, Maddy reappeared. 'Burns Books will be open, won't it?'

'I should think so, yes. Why?'

'Oh, I fancied an espresso. I expect Em will have the machine on by now.'

'Why don't you head over, then.' She figured there was no point trying to stop Maddy. She already looked like a woman on a mission, and standing in her way could well lead to a row. *I hope this isn't too obvious to Luke*, she thought. *And I really hope Lennox Nash isn't in yet. He'd love this.*

With barely an acknowledgement, Maddy was already half out of the door. She hadn't even stopped to express any disapproval of the cats, who were curled up by the radiator. *How soon things change.* Jemma sighed, and began to load coins into the till.

When Maddy returned half an hour later, flushed, eyes sparkling, and with a book-shaped lump visible in her bag, Jemma was reading a book on gemstones. 'Did you enjoy your espresso?' she asked. 'I thought you'd bring it back with you.'

Maddy had the grace to be flustered. 'Oh, sorry.'

'How are things there? All OK?'

'Oh yes. Dr Nash said he had a lovely weekend going for long country walks and reading beside roaring log fires.' She gazed over Jemma's shoulder, possibly at an imaginary roaring log fire. Then she snapped back to the present. 'How was your weekend?'

'I've had better. Carl is taking his play on tour, and he left yesterday.'

Maddy actually seemed to take this in. 'Oh, I didn't know. I'm sorry.'

'It's fine, he'll only be gone for a few months.'

'Like Raphael,' said Maddy.

'I suppose.' Jemma looked down at the book. She had identified the purple stone in her bracelet as an amethyst. According to the book, amethysts protected against negative energy, brought peace, and helped to keep the wearer balanced and put their thoughts into action. *That's something*, she thought, touching the small purple bead with her forefinger. As for the yellow stone, she couldn't make up her mind whether it was topaz, carnelian, chalcedony, or citrine. She wasn't even sure whether those were different stones. It could wait, though. If Lennox was at Burns Books – and he almost certainly was – she had a whole other investigation to do. 'I'd better see whether Dr Nash wants to brief me on anything,' she said, closing the book and rising.

Maddy's brow furrowed slightly. 'He didn't mention anything. I'm sure he would have told me.'

'All right, I confess,' said Jemma. 'It's your fault, Maddy, for mentioning coffee. I was doing fine before that, but now I fancy a cappuccino.'

'Oh!' exclaimed Maddy, and giggled. 'That's all right then.'

'I won't be long,' said Jemma. She was about to say *Call me if you need me* when she remembered that wasn't an option. She had tried her phone as soon as Maddy had left the shop, and again there had been no signal.

'Aren't we popular,' Luke said, as soon as she walked through the door of Burns Books. 'First Maddy, now you. Although neither of you came to see me, of course.'

'How are you, Luke?' Jemma said hastily. 'Did you have a good weekend?'

'Not especially.' She could tell. Luke looked as if he had slept in his clothes, which were less smart and dashing than usual, and he definitely hadn't shaved. His eyes seemed deeper set than usual, and there were dark marks underneath them.

'I'm sorry,' she said. 'Me neither. Carl moved out.' Luke glanced up at her with the recognition of a fellow sufferer. 'It's temporary, but… He's off around the country with his play.'

'Oh, I see.' His head drooped. 'If you're after the lord and master, he's downstairs with his adoring fans. Half of London wants to meet him.' His own expression suggested he would prefer Lennox Nash to be as far away as possible.

'I'll just pop down,' said Jemma. 'I've got something to ask him.'

As she headed for the staircase, she heard the hum of voices. It grew stronger as she descended. When she opened the great oak door to the lower floor, the noise swarmed round her.

Lennox was standing in the centre of a crowd of people at least five deep on every side. Only his height made him visible. He was smiling graciously, shaking hands, and signing the occasional autograph.

As she moved closer, she could hear him. 'Yes, copies of my latest book will arrive in a few days. In the meantime, why not browse the shelves? I probably shouldn't, but I'm willing to sign other people's books.' He said this with a grin which made Jemma feel as if someone were scraping their nails down a blackboard. She swallowed, and drew closer.

He caught sight of her. 'Ah, Jemma, good to see you. Did you order that sandwich board?'

Is that all you can think about? Jemma indicated the crowd. 'Given how many people have come to see you, Dr Nash, I hardly think we need to advertise further.'

He looked like a cat who had got the cream. 'That is true. Would you mind hopping on the till? I'm sure lots of people are more than ready to buy a book.'

As soon as he said those words, the crowd surged towards the shelves. Some made for a specific section and stood, pondering, while others ran to the nearest shelf and grabbed a book at random before dashing to the counter.

Jemma raised her eyebrows at Em, standing idle in the café, and received the tiniest shrug in response. She hurried to the shop counter and picked up the scanner. Meanwhile, Lennox sauntered to a table, sat down, and took out his fountain pen.

The next hour was a blur of scanning books and taking payment. At least no one wanted a bag: it would have impeded their dash to join the queue for the famous Lennox Nash. Jemma could just see him, having a brief word with each customer as he signed the title page of their book. But one thing puzzled her. *If he's famous enough to bring customers flocking to the shop, how come I haven't heard of him?*

Eventually, Lennox stood up. 'I'm afraid I must leave,' he announced. 'I have to see a man about a book.' He put his pen in his pocket, and began shaking the hands of the people still in the queue.

The customers waiting to pay for their books immediately abandoned them on the nearest surface. *So much for that,* thought Jemma. Then she remembered why she had come to the bookshop in the first place. She left the counter and met Lennox as he worked his way down the line. 'Dr Nash, before you go, how were things at the London Library on Saturday?'

'Oh, fine, fine,' he said, still smiling at the customers.

'What sort of emergency was it? If you like, I can sort out the paperwork for you. I don't mind, honestly.'

'Already done,' he said, still not looking at her. 'Barely worth calling an emergency.' He quickened his pace, pumping hands, until he came to the end of the queue. 'Must dash, everyone, but I shall return, never fear!'

'When will you be back, Dr Nash? Just so that we know, for cover.'

'When you see me.' He turned to the customers, grinning. 'She does fuss terribly,' he said, and they all laughed.

The rush over, Jemma returned to the Friendly Bookshop sunk in gloom. She had obtained little new information from Lennox about the knowledge emergency, and worse, somehow he had managed to entice customers to the shop simply by being there. She kicked a pebble along the pavement, feeling thoroughly useless.

Maddy was sitting at the counter, not even hiding the fact that she was reading *Wuthering Heights*. 'I take it it's been busy,' said Jemma.

'Monday morning,' said Maddy, with a shrug. 'What do you expect?' The shop phone rang but she didn't bother to pick it up, already immersed in her book.

'I'll get that, shall I?' Jemma walked to the counter, picked up the receiver and put it to her ear, fully expecting an annoying request from Lennox. 'Good morning, the Friendly Bookshop.'

'Jemma, is that you?' It was Jasper Bantam's voice. 'I called your mobile, but it doesn't seem to be working.'

'Oh, hello.' Jemma cast a furtive glance at Maddy, but she was presumably out on the moors. 'What can I do for you?'

'I wondered if you'd like that drink and chat. I'm free for the next hour if that suits you.'

An hour or so would take her nicely to Maddy's lunch break. 'Yes, I can fit that in.'

'Super. I'll see you at the Archibald Hotel.'

'I'll come now. Bye.' She put the phone down, which made Maddy look up. 'Supplier problems,' said Jemma, making for the door.

'Oh, OK.' Maddy returned to her book. Jemma suspected it would take an earthquake or the unexpected arrival of Lennox Nash to make her stop reading. But she was already on her way to the Archibald Hotel.

Chapter 12

When Jemma reached the Archibald Hotel, she gazed up at it doubtfully. *Did he really mean here?* It looked fancy. Very fancy, and therefore expensive. However, when she ventured up the steps, into the lobby, and through to the restaurant, Jasper was sitting at a table by the window. She waved, though she wasn't sure if that was etiquette, and walked over. He stood up as she approached, which made her feel rather grand.

'This is nice,' she said. That was an understatement. The restaurant had a high ceiling painted with classical scenes, large windows, posh silky wallpaper, and a mixture of big round tables and snug little ones. Jasper had chosen one of the snug little ones with a view onto the street. She wondered if he had seen her hesitating outside the hotel, and felt her face warm up. *It's not my fault*, she thought, leaning over to put her bag down and surreptitiously putting her hands on her cheeks to cool them. *I've never been somewhere like this.* She dreaded to think how much even a pot of tea would cost, and hoped Jasper wasn't expecting to split the bill.

'It's lovely, isn't it?' said Jasper. 'I don't come here often, but I wanted to meet you somewhere nice.' Jemma was convinced that her face must be scarlet by now. Carl had never taken her anywhere remotely like this. 'I would have ordered for you, but I wasn't sure what you'd prefer. They have quite a range, but the tea sommelier can advise you.' He indicated a dinner-jacketed person standing at the side of the room.

'The tea sommelier,' Jemma repeated. If someone hadn't been standing there, she would have thought Jasper was making fun of her. She eyed the dainty silver tea service in front of Jasper. 'What did you order?'

'English Breakfast,' said Jasper, looking a little embarrassed. 'I'm afraid I'm rather traditional when it comes to tea.'

'In that case, I'll join you,' said Jemma, greatly relieved. A waiter was at their side in a moment, and she placed her order.

'An excellent choice, madam,' he said gravely, and she felt oddly gratified.

Once he had left, she turned back to Jasper. 'So, how did the emergency go on Saturday?'

A wary look came over Jasper's face. 'Oh, it was all sorted out. I must admit I was surprised when a stranger came into the library. I was expecting you, you see.'

'Dr Nash, you mean?' said Jemma. 'How did you find him?'

'Oh, he was very pleasant and obviously extremely capable. I was just taken unawares. All I could gather was that he was filling in for Raphael.' He frowned. 'Where is Raphael?'

'He's on a sort of secondment in Italy,' Jemma replied. This wasn't going as she had planned. She had imagined a careful interrogation of Jasper with some note-taking, plenty of nodding, and a gradual revelation of the detail surrounding the knowledge emergency.

Jasper's eyes widened. 'Raphael's on secondment? That's never happened before. I didn't think he'd ever leave the bookshop. Why has he gone?'

'A change is as good as a rest,' said Jemma. 'He's away for a few months. Do tell me about the emergency, Jasper. What kind of book was it?'

'Your English Breakfast tea, madam,' said the waiter, making Jemma jump. He was bearing a tray laden with silver and china. 'And as you are a new guest, we have included a plate of complimentary biscuits.'

'Oh, thank you.' Jemma silently cursed the waiter for interrupting at a crucial moment. Now there was silverware to arrange and tea to pour, not to mention biscuits. Then again, biscuits were always welcome, especially in moments of crisis.

'So this chap Nash is a doctor?' asked Jasper. 'What sort of doctor? He just introduced himself to me as Lennox and said he was popping in on his way somewhere.'

'Raphael introduced him to me as Dr Nash,' said Jemma. 'I believe he's an academic, among other things. We were on an interview panel together, you see, before he came into post.'

'An interview panel?' Jasper's eyes widened. 'Has a

new post been advertised?' He looked put out.

'In Berkshire,' said Jemma, 'not here.'

'Oh.' Jasper drank some tea. 'Forgive my curiosity, but the workings of the Keepers' Guild are rather, well, shadowy, and it's always interesting to learn more.' He sipped his tea. 'I thought you meant Raphael's job. From what I understand, he has been in post for a considerable time.'

Jemma wondered if Jasper knew exactly how long Raphael had been the Keeper of books for England. 'No, this was entirely different.' She sipped her own tea, which was lovely. 'So, back to this book. You said on the phone that it was attracting other books?'

'Yes, it was most peculiar,' said Jasper. 'One of our members brought it to my attention. She was trying to take a book from the shelf, but when she pulled it out, four other books came with it. She tried to prise them apart, but couldn't. Naturally she assumed that glue had got on the books, perhaps from the binding. She brought it to the attention of an assistant, who summoned me. Unfortunately, he had put the books on a trolley, and by the time I arrived all the books on that shelf were welded together. That was when I rang you.'

'I see.' Admittedly, Jemma hadn't worked her way through all the possible book-emergency scenarios, but she had never heard of one where books stuck to each other. 'But you didn't think it was serious.'

'Well, no,' said Jasper. 'It was nothing like the situation you resolved for us. No heat, no smoke, no rumbling…'

'What did Dr Nash do, if you don't mind me asking?'

'I felt an utter fool, I must admit. After I had explained the situation, he simply strode up to the trolley and pulled out the middle book. The other books fell apart from each other as if they'd never been stuck. I even wondered if we had imagined it.'

'How strange. Did he explain?'

'He just said it was one of those things.' Jasper looked puzzled. Then his attention returned to Jemma, and he smiled. 'Are you enjoying your tea?'

'Very much, thank you. Would you like a biscuit?'

'If you're sure you don't mind,' said Jasper. 'Have you had one yet? You should, they're superb.'

Jemma sampled a biscuit. It was shortbread, with a crest in the middle, and as Jasper had said, it was superb. 'Mmm,' she said, conscious of crumbs.

'These are possibly my favourite biscuits,' said Jasper. 'So, what is Raphael doing in Italy? I assume it must be important to make him leave his position and the bookshop. And you.'

Jemma was about to retort that she could manage perfectly well, thank you, when she understood from the slight flush on Jasper's cheeks that he had been paying her a compliment, and her own face heated up as if in sympathy. 'I don't know what he's doing, to be honest,' she said quickly. 'It's all been rather a whirl, what with Raphael leaving and Dr Nash coming and – personal things.' She had been about to say, 'and Carl moving out.'

'Oh, I'm sorry,' said Jasper, immediately looking concerned. 'Have you had bad news?'

'Not as such,' Jemma replied. 'In fact, you could say

it's good news. My boyfriend's play has been so successful that he's taking it on tour, but that means he won't be around for a few months.'

'Oh,' said Jasper. He leaned forward. 'That's splendid, for him. But if you ever need someone to, um, go to the theatre with, I could be available.'

Jemma had a terrible urge to giggle, which she fought valiantly. 'That's very kind, Jasper, but I'll be fine. If I do find myself at a loose end, I'll give you a call.'

'But your phone's out of action, isn't it?' asked Jasper.

'It has been temperamental lately,' said Jemma. 'I think it's time for a new one. I'll make sure you have my new number.' *That'll fox Lennox Nash*, she thought, with pleasure.

'Oh yes, do,' said Jasper. 'It was unsettling earlier, when I couldn't get through on the phone. I wondered if something had happened to you. I asked Lennox where you were when he turned up at the library, but he just said you were otherwise engaged.'

Jemma stored this away for future reference. 'I'm sorry if the phone thing worried you. I'll definitely get that sorted.' *This lunchtime, if possible.* 'So, what was the book at the centre of the drama?'

Jasper took another biscuit. 'I don't actually know. You see, none of us knew that book *was* causing the problem until Dr Nash arrived, and he removed the book so quickly that none of us saw. All I can tell you is that it was small, dark red, and slightly battered. It had gold lettering, but most of that was worn off. It didn't look like one of our books; they're usually in better—'

Jemma's mobile shrilled and they both jumped. 'Excuse me a moment,' said Jemma, fishing in her bag. The display showed a number she didn't recognise. She debated whether to answer it, but the fact of the phone working during shop hours was enough to convince her. 'Hello?'

'Ah, hello Jemma,' said Lennox. 'Sorry to bother you, as I'm sure you're busy at the bookshop, but I thought it best to phone you directly. Luke said he couldn't get through, but he must have misdialled.'

'Oh,' said Jemma. 'What can I do for you, Dr Nash?'

'Another emergency has come up.' His tone was very smooth.

'*Another* one?'

'Yes. A serious one, from the sound of it. The unfortunate thing is that I've just left Paddington. Visiting Sarah in Reading to make sure she's settled in, you know. So I'm afraid you'll have to step up. Normally I'd take charge of the emergency, especially since you're rather green, but hopefully you'll be able to contain matters till I return.'

Contain matters? What on earth is going on?

'It's at the Maughan Library on Chancery Lane, and I strongly suggest you get a cab. We're about to go through a tun—' The call ended.

'Is that what I think it is?' said Jasper. He looked extremely apprehensive.

'If you think it's another knowledge emergency, you're exactly right,' Jemma replied, stowing the phone in her bag.

Jasper swallowed. 'I could come with you…'

'It'll be fine,' said Jemma. 'I've handled a Grade One emergency, remember?' She tried to smile, but it wouldn't stay in place. 'Thanks for the tea; it was lovely. Maybe we can do it again some time.'

'Yes, that would be nice,' said Jasper, but the worry hadn't left his face. 'Please call me later and let me know you're all right, won't you?' He put a hand on hers and squeezed it.

'I'd better go,' said Jemma. She got up, her hand still in Jasper's, and he released it reluctantly. 'I promise I'll phone.' She didn't want to say goodbye – she'd had enough of goodbyes lately – so she left it at that.

A taxi was waiting outside with its light on. 'Maughan Library, please.' And as the taxi's engine rumbled, Jemma wondered what on earth she would find this time.

Chapter 13

'Are you sure this is it?' asked Jemma, as the taxi grumbled to a halt at an archway with wrought-iron gates.

The taxi driver twisted round. 'You saying I don't know my way round London?'

'Of course not,' said Jemma. 'It's just…' *Scarier than I thought it would be,* she admitted, in her head. She couldn't even see the library yet, but she had driven past enough impressive stone buildings to be very, very worried.

'I thought you were a student,' said the cabbie. 'Anyway, are you getting out or what? I'll be charging you waiting time soon.'

Jemma fumbled in her bag, found her purse, and touched her card to the reader. 'Want a receipt?' asked the driver. He sounded friendlier now that she'd paid.

'Yes please,' said Jemma. She could claim it as expenses; after all, Lennox had told her to take a taxi. *That's assuming I get out of this alive.* She got down from the cab, closed the door firmly, and walked towards the railings.

Oh no. Through the archway Jemma saw a courtyard, trees, and at the far end, a large stone building – and the closer she walked, the bigger it got. It was like a cathedral, with mellow stone, lots and lots of windows, and a tower above the entrance. That was bad enough, but what was worse was that people were leaving the building. Some merely walked quickly, but others ran, looking back every so often at the building as if it might follow.

She didn't want to go in, but she had to – assuming she could get past the flow of people coming the other way. She had hoped to sneak in behind somebody, but nobody was entering the library. Jemma waited for the flow to ease, listening to the snatches of conversation as people passed:

'I thought they were filming at first.'

'I don't understand what was happening in there.'

'The librarian rang 999 and asked for all the emergency services.'

Jemma swallowed and pushed forward, trying not to elbow people as she fought her way into the library. Once she had got through the crowd, though, she encountered another obstacle.

'I'm sorry, you can't come in.' The speaker was a short, broad man with a purple lanyard round his neck. 'We're evacuating the library.'

'Why, what's going on?'

He huffed. 'If we knew that, we probably wouldn't need to evacuate.' He stepped back to let another scurrying group through. 'Trust me, you won't get any learning done with things the way they are.' His eyes narrowed. 'Can I see your ID card, please?'

Jemma moved to the side and pretended to rummage in her bag. *What should I do? I have to get in, and there's no way they'll let me.*

Then she thought of something. It worked on books, but she had no idea if it would work on people. She raised her head, looked the man in the eye, and said quietly, 'I am an Assistant Keeper, and I am here to help.'

'What?' The man cupped his ear. 'I'm sorry, I can't hear a thing with this clattering.'

Jemma tried again, this time sending the message silently. *I am an Assistant Keeper.*

Understanding began to dawn on the man's face, but a young female student ran between them, gabbling into her phone, and the connection was broken.

'For heaven's sake,' muttered Jemma. She walked right up to the man and fixed him with her hardest stare. 'I am an Assistant Keeper.'

He retreated a couple of steps, staring back at her. 'It's in the Round Reading Room. Well, it isn't round really, but close enough. You'll see. Don't say I didn't warn you. Turn right, and it's on your left, past the stairs. I'd tell you to follow the shouting, but it's everywhere.'

Jemma took the direction he had indicated. There were fewer students in the corridor, probably because most had already left, but her pace grew slower and slower. It felt as if waves of panic and terror were pulsing down the corridor. Belatedly, she realised she had no equipment with her: no tongs, no gloves, no mask, no lead-lined box, no book chains.

'What am I going to do?' she whispered.

A little voice in her head said, *You are an Assistant Keeper, and you will sort things out.*

I'm glad you're so sure of that, she replied, but nevertheless, she felt better. *I am an Assistant Keeper. I am an Assistant Keeper.* She was saying the words aloud, but it didn't matter. No one was listening.

At last she came to the door of the Round Reading Room. A few people were peeping in, jaws slack. 'Excuse me,' said Jemma, and went in.

Normally, it would have been a beautiful room. It was, as the man had said, round or nearly so, lined with bookshelves and topped with a glass dome. But today it inspired fear, not wonder. At the top of the dome, black smoke was gathering. The lights were out, and the room was darkening every second. Near the door stood two librarians, conferring and gazing upwards, their heads moving from side to side as though they were watching an erratic bird in flight.

In a way, they were. A book was ricocheting around the room, striking railings and desks, rebounding from the dome and bouncing off the carpet. Every time it made an impact, another plume of black smoke rose from the place it had hit. It looked as if the library were on fire, but there were no flames: just smoke.

Jemma tapped one of the librarians on the arm. She whipped round, an angry expression on her face. 'You startled me! What do you want?'

'I'm an Assistant Keeper,' said Jemma. 'I'm here to

help.'

'An Assistant Keeper? What good is that? Look at it! Look at what it's doing!' She pointed at the book, which continued to whizz around the library. If anything, it was picking up momentum. She coughed, then found a handkerchief and put it to her mouth.

'That's a good idea,' said Jemma. She dug in her pocket but found only tissues. She remembered her scarf, which she had left at the Friendly Bookshop in her haste to meet Jasper. *I should have stopped on the way*, she thought. *I should have picked up the kitbag.* But it was too late now. She would have to manage. She shrugged off her coat and held it in front of her face.

The librarian who had spoken to her tapped her arm. 'Where is the Keeper?'

'I'm afraid he's on a train,' said Jemma. *Why has he left me to do this alone? According to Jasper, the emergency at the London Library was minor. Why did Lennox keep me away from that, then plunge me into this?*

The first answer that came to her didn't bear thinking about. She blinked, and her eyes began to itch. Things were getting worse, not better.

She removed the coat from her face, lifted her head, and addressed the book. 'I am an Assistant Keeper,' she cried, 'and I command you to stop what you are doing.'

The book continued to thump and crash. She had no idea what was driving it, but she didn't like it at all.

'Please stop what you are doing,' she said, in slightly more measured tones. 'This is a library: a place of learning.'

The pace of the book slowed, and it moved from high in the dome to the top shelves.

The other librarian tapped her arm. 'Excuse me,' she said. 'Are you accredited?'

The book picked up speed.

'Look what you've done!' said the first librarian. 'Just when we were getting somewhere.' She shook her fist at the book. 'You have no business behaving in this manner. In a library, of all places!'

The book whizzed past the librarian's nose and she jumped back. It rebounded against the shelf, fell to the floor as if it had been stunned, then bounced into the dome.

Jemma heard a crack. 'Oh no, the glass!' cried the first librarian.

'Never mind the glass,' said the second librarian, pointing. 'Look at that.'

Now two books were banging their way round the library. Then there were three, then four.

This is like the Sorcerer's Apprentice, thought Jemma. *Or some horrible nightmare. In fact, both.* She faced the librarians. 'Quiet, please.' She saw a sign. 'Be respectful of others.'

The first librarian's eyes almost fell out of her head with rage, but she closed her mouth.

Jemma took a step forward, though she had no idea what to do. She even found herself wishing that Lennox had come. *He could probably raise his hand and stop this. Or Raphael could, of course. What can I do? I'm only an Assistant Keeper.* She looked up at the books, whizzing through the air like an army of vicious birds bent on destruction. *Thwack. Thwack. Thwack.* She took a deep breath. *But they aren't here and I am, so it's my job.*

She considered ringing Lennox for advice. Then again, what was the point? She probably wouldn't be able to get hold of him, and if she did, he would either fob her off or assume knowledge that she didn't have.

A book hit the dome with a crash, followed by a shower of glass. Another book flew upwards through the gap, and vanished.

'Oh no!' shrieked the first librarian. 'The books are escaping! Do something!'

Jemma's brain whirled. The situation was worsening; that went without saying. The thought of the books fleeing the library and going who knew where, to do who knew what, was terrifying.

She had two priorities: stop the books hitting other books, and get them to slow down, if not stop. She lifted her head to the dome. 'What is it?' she cried. 'What's wrong?'

'Can't you see what's wrong?' said the second librarian, staring at her as if she were out of her senses.

'I'm not talking to you,' said Jemma, still looking up. 'I'm talking to the books. Tell me what's wrong. Tell me why you're so upset.'

A book hit her on the arm and plopped to the floor. Jemma bit her lip to stop herself crying out, then picked the book up. *The Effective Manager*, she read. *I should give this a try; I could certainly use some help.* Instead, she handed it to the nearest librarian. 'Can you check this for damage and make sure it's shelved in the right place, please.'

The librarian took the book and stared at it. 'That shouldn't even be in here.'

'Ow!' Jemma cried, as a book whacked her on the shoulder and fell.

The librarian retrieved it. '*Prioritisation for Beginners*,' she read, and shrugged.

Jemma stared at her as realisation dawned. *This is meant for me.* She pulled her coat on, put her hood up, took her gloves from her pockets, and stared upwards. The books were slowing down.

'Tell me what's wrong,' she said, in a normal voice, and braced herself.

A book hit her elbow, giving her pins and needles in her arm, but it dropped to the floor like the others. 'Tell me what the title is,' Jemma said quietly.

'*Running A Successful Business*,' said the librarian.

The next book caught her on the back of the knee. '*How To Win Friends And Influence People*,' read the librarian. 'Tanya, would you mind fetching that trolley?'

The other librarian hurried off. Jemma could hear her footsteps, but dared not look away from the books. The next one hit her on the hand. It didn't break the skin, but there would be a bruise later. In the meantime it had left a sooty black mark, but the thumping and clanging was slowing.

Just a few books were left. Jemma steeled herself. 'Why are you upset?' She covered her head as the rest of the books rained down on her, then fell to the floor.

The library was silent, and she opened her eyes. The only signs of what had occurred were the cold air coming from the broken panes high above, the glass on the floor, the books surrounding her, and the plumes of sooty smoke rising towards the hole in the dome.

She lowered her hands, and nothing happened. 'I think it's over,' she said, and turned to the librarians, who were both staring at her.

'What was that?' one of them said, scowling. 'Are there hidden cameras? Was this some sort of joke?'

'That was no joke,' said Jemma, as a group of police in riot gear burst through the door.

They pulled up short when they saw the three figures. 'What's been going on?' said the one in the lead, lowering his baton. 'Why is a member of the public in here? And why is she so filthy?'

The librarians stepped back. 'Your guess is as good as mine,' said the first librarian. 'She forced her way in, and things got worse.'

'Then they got better,' said Jemma. 'I stopped it. You *saw* me.'

The policeman moved forward swiftly and took Jemma's arm. 'The man on the door doesn't think you're even a member of the university,' he said, his nose wrinkling at the acrid smell of smoke. At least, Jemma hoped that was what it was. 'You've got some explaining to do.'

Chapter 14

When the radio woke Jemma with the London news the next morning, she groaned. Halfway through, she groaned again and put the covers over her head, but she couldn't block it out.

'Mystery surrounds strange goings-on at a university library yesterday. The Maughan Library, part of King's College London, was seemingly invaded by a poltergeist, or possibly two. Onlookers reported that books were flinging themselves around the library, even smashing glass in the great dome. Students and staff were forced to evacuate.'

Jemma exhaled cautiously.

'However, there were also reports of an interloper in the building. Given the library's popularity as a filming location, this could have been a publicity stunt. The police were called, but no one has been charged.'

Still cowering under the covers, Jemma wondered whether to call in sick. *I'll have to face it sometime.* She threw off the duvet, which prompted a disapproving squeak from Luna, and went to the bathroom, where she discovered that her period was right on time. 'Wonderful,' she muttered.

Some of yesterday was still a little blurry. She had been taken to a study room by the policeman in charge, a tough-looking man with cropped dark hair and beady brown eyes who introduced himself as Sergeant Hawkins, and invited to give her version of events. *Where do I begin?* she thought. How on earth could she attempt to explain her part in subduing the books – if inviting books to throw themselves at you could be described as subduing. In an attempt to play for time, Jemma had asked for a glass of water, and the next thing she remembered was being helped up from the floor.

'Nothing anyone's said makes any sense,' said Sergeant Hawkins, whose demeanour had softened considerably. 'I suspect you're suffering from the effects of smoke inhalation, and it probably isn't just you.' He pinched the bridge of his nose. 'You're unfit to give a statement at present. Give me your name and contact details, and we'll worry about statements later.'

A member of staff came in and gave her a cup of tea which, when she sipped it, was revoltingly sweet. 'What time is it?' Jemma asked. 'I must get back to the shop. My assistant will wonder where I am.'

'Your assistant can manage without you for the afternoon,' said Sergeant Hawkins. 'In fact, I'm not sure I should let you go home. You should probably get checked over at the hospital.'

Jemma shook her head and winced. 'Exactly,' said the

police officer. 'Drink that tea, then get on and ring somebody to take you home. I have other things to do besides look after you, you know.' But he said it kindly.

Jemma gulped down her tea to get it over with, and considered who to ring. Her parents were too far away, and the thought of the inevitable explanations was terrifying. Carl, no doubt, was busy being important, and therefore unreachable. Maddy, Luke and Em would be tied up at the bookshops. Lennox – *no*.

For a moment Jemma felt very alone. Then a name came to her. They weren't on those terms . . . but he *had* asked her to phone him afterwards. She just hadn't imagined it being like this.

She pulled her phone from her bag, then remembered. 'Is there a phone in the library I could use? Mine is nearly out of charge.'

Sergeant Hawkins said nothing, but pulled a phone from his pocket and handed it to her. 'Thank you,' said Jemma. She found Jasper's name in her contacts, and dialled.

'Good afternoon, Jasper Bantam.'

'Oh, hi Jasper, it's Jemma.'

'Jemma!' He sounded genuinely pleased to hear her voice. 'Did it go all right?'

She was conscious of Sergeant Hawkins sitting a few feet away. 'It's over, but . . . I hurt myself. Nothing serious, just bruises, but they won't let me leave unless someone goes with me. I'm really sorry to ask you, but we're short-staffed at the bookshop, and—'

'Where are you? I'll get a taxi.'

'I'm at the Maughan Library on Chancery Lane. I don't know if they'll let you in.'

'I'll get in. You stay there.' In the background, a door closed. 'I'm on my way.'

The call ended and Jemma handed back the phone. Things seemed to be moving very quickly. *Was that the right thing to do?* She had no idea, but at least Jasper was coming and she would be able to leave soon. She just hoped Jasper would be discreet, and not raise more questions in Sergeant Hawkins's mind.

Another police officer stuck his head round the door of the study room, and the sergeant joined him. They had a muttered conversation, during which the sergeant glanced at Jemma every so often. Finally, with an 'All right then,' the other officer departed.

Sergeant Hawkins walked back to her. 'It's still a mess, but it looks as if you're in the clear, young lady. The only thing those two librarians could agree on was that the business with the flying books had been going on for at least half an hour before you came on the scene. Otherwise, they might as well have been describing two different incidents.' He sighed. 'I have no idea what's been happening today, but I don't like it. And I still don't understand what you were doing here.' His expression was slightly baleful. 'Who's coming to fetch you?'

'Jasper Bantam.'

The sergeant snorted. 'Jasper Bantam, eh? That his real name?'

'He's a senior member of staff at the London Library. I'm sure he'll have some ID.'

'Right.' He unclipped a radio from his belt and spoke into it. 'A Jasper Bantam will be arriving shortly. Take him round the back and keep him away from the press.'

'The press?' Jemma's head swam.

'What do you expect? Loads of students with phones. I bet there are a hundred videos up on YouTube already, not to mention Instagram. Everyone's into that these days.'

Jemma put her head in her hands. She only hoped it had been too dark in the library for anyone to film her with the books.

***

Jasper looked visibly distressed when he saw her. 'Jemma, are you all right? What happened?'

'I got hit by a lot of books,' said Jemma. 'I've got a slight headache.'

'I'm not surprised. Can you stand? Do you need a doctor?'

'No doctors,' said Jemma. 'I'm fine; I'm probably just tired.'

'I've got a taxi outside,' said Jasper. 'I'll take you home.'

She was too overcome at the thought of finally leaving the library to do more than murmur her thanks.

Sergeant Hawkins took them to the back entrance and handed them over to another officer. 'Make sure no one gets at her,' he said. 'She'll give us a statement when she's ready.' He handed Jemma a business card. 'Here's my number. I'll be in touch soon, anyway.'

'Thank you,' said Jemma, but he was already heading inside. She huddled in her coat as if shielding herself from questions, but Jasper took her arm and steered her expertly to the taxi. She wondered whether he had ever done anything like this before.

'Come on, let's get you home,' he said, and helped her in. 'Where is home?'

She felt her cheeks flushing. 'I live in the flat above the Friendly Bookshop on Charing Cross Road.'

'Ah.' He gave the address to the driver and sat back. 'I won't ask you any questions; you've clearly had enough.'

'I'd better go into the bookshop first,' said Jemma. 'Poor Maddy will be starving.'

'Never mind Maddy,' said Jasper. 'I'll take you upstairs, then talk to Maddy. I'm sure she can cope.'

When they reached the shop, he helped her out, paid the fare – Jemma was too embarrassed to look at the meter – and assisted her in finding her keys and opening the door. 'I can manage, really I can,' she said. 'You don't need to come up.'

'I *do* need to make sure you get upstairs safely,' he replied. 'Now come along.'

Meekly, Jemma complied. It was rather nice being taken charge of for once. She unlocked the door of the flat and the cats came to greet her.

'Will you be all right from here?' asked Jasper. 'Should I, um, take you upstairs?'

'I'll be fine,' Jemma said quickly. 'Thank you so much for your help, Jasper. I'll take some paracetamol and get to bed.'

'That's a good idea. Maybe take a bath first. Aches and pains, you know. If you need anything, call me. I'll go now.' He pulled the door closed behind him.

Jemma let her bag drop to the floor. She could just see the cats' bowls in the corner of the kitchen area: Luna's was empty. 'You're eating me out of house and home,' she told Luna as she refilled both bowls.

Luna purred and began to eat, waving her tail.

'Maybe I should ask the vet about putting you on a diet,' said Jemma, and embarked on the painful journey upstairs to bed.

She was halfway into her pyjamas before she remembered that Jasper had mentioned a bath. She moved slowly to the bathroom and gasped at the sight of herself in the mirror. She looked as if she had emerged from a house fire. Her normally reddish-brown hair was dark with smoke, her face smeared with soot. She stumbled to the shower, turned it on, and started to get out of her clothes. *I needn't have worried about him coming upstairs,* she thought, wincing as she touched a bruise. *He probably couldn't wait to leave.*

***

When Jemma went down to open the Friendly Bookshop the following morning, Maddy was already standing outside. 'I wasn't sure if you were coming in today,' she said. 'That man didn't say.'

'That man, Maddy, was Jasper Bantam, and he very kindly brought me home after a book-related incident. I've had plenty of sleep, and I'm fine.'

'Mmm,' said Maddy.

'What do you mean, mmm?'

'Oh, nothing.' Maddy retreated behind the counter and

opened a book catalogue.

At nine o'clock precisely, the bookshop phone rang. For a wonder, Maddy answered it. 'Good morning, the Friendly Bookshop,' she said, in an annoying singsong voice. 'Oh hello, Dr Nash. Yes of course… Yes, I'll tell her… See you later, maybe. Bye.'

She put down the phone. 'Dr Nash wants to see you at Burns Books immediately.'

***

'In short, Jemma, your conduct yesterday was foolhardy, attention-seeking, and worst of all, unprofessional.' At least Lennox had taken her to the stockroom for her telling-off, though she suspected it would be audible to any customer who cared to listen.

'What was I meant to do? I arrived and found the situation completely out of control—'

'I don't care. If you couldn't manage the situation, you should have retreated and phoned me.'

'But you were on a train—'

'Rule One for a knowledge emergency of any grade: do not engage with a situation beyond your competence. The first rule – the *cardinal* rule – and you disobeyed it.'

'I fixed it, though. I calmed the books down.'

'At what cost?' Lennox paced the stockroom floor. 'We don't even know that yet. The only saving grace in this mess is that somehow you got out without breaching the secrecy of the Guild. That, I am sure, was accidental.' He rounded on her. 'Don't forget that you are on probation, Jemma. I shall be putting this on file, and taking it further if necessary. If you were my employee…' Jemma felt a surge of relief that she wasn't.

His sea-green glare pinned her to the spot. It was like being roasted by the sun through a magnifying glass. 'I suggest you restart your training from the very beginning. There are clearly serious gaps in your comprehension.' He stared down his nose at her. 'That is all. For now.'

Jemma left the stockroom and hurried to the door, feeling ten centimetres tall. Before she could leave, though, Luke whipped round the counter and intercepted her.

'It was on the news,' he said. 'I saw videos on social media, too. I don't care what *he* says; you must have done a good job to sort that out. It looked fierce.'

'Thanks,' muttered Jemma, her cheeks warming all over again. It was becoming a habit.

'Ignore him; he dumped it on you because he didn't want to miss his jolly. I heard him say he was meeting someone on the phone—' Abruptly, he walked back behind the counter.

A second later, the stockroom door opened and Lennox strode out. Jemma, though, was already fleeing to avoid a second scolding. *The more distance between him and me*, she thought as she half-ran down the street, *the better.*

Chapter 15

For the next few days, Jemma kept a very low profile. When she wasn't working at the Friendly Bookshop she kept to her flat, except for occasional forays to Nafisa's mini market for basic food supplies. Even then, she wore a hat and a pair of glasses with plain lenses which Carl had left behind. The last thing she needed was for somebody who had been at the Maughan Library to point a finger and shriek 'That's her!'

She actually spent her first evening confined to the flat doing what Lennox had suggested: going through her training notes. But try as she might, she could find nothing which applied to the situation at the Maughan Library. Books smoking: yes. Bursting into flames: yes. Playing book-pong and infecting other books? That was unprecedented. And it had been meant for her. 'Someone wants to get me,' she whispered. As far as she was concerned, the finger pointed squarely at Lennox Nash. He would know the Maughan Library, as an academic and scholar. He had taken care to have an appointment outside the area, so that he couldn't deal with it. He could have asked another Assistant Keeper to deal with the emergency: a more experienced one who knew the area and the library. But no, he had forced her to go. 'It was definitely him,' she muttered. 'But why?'

Luna looked up from her cushion and gave a tiny meow.

'Even if that's the right answer, I don't speak cat,' Jemma replied.

Luna stood up and stretched, then jumped down and wandered to the kitchen area. Shortly afterwards, Jemma heard crunching. *She's put on weight.* She sighed, and set a reminder on her new phone to ring the vet.

The one thing she had managed to succeed in, apart from staying under the radar, was buying a new pay-as-you-go phone. She had tested it by texting her new number to her parents and her sister, Carl, Luke, Em, Raphael, and Jasper during work hours. Not to Maddy, from whom she kept the phone well hidden and in silent mode.

Most people had replied to her text, which made Jemma feel a little less alone. The exceptions were Raphael and Jasper. Carl's message had been brief. *Thanks sorry can't talk now, at a tricky point. Speak tonight? C x*. But when she rang him the call went to voicemail, and he still hadn't called her back. She tried not to think about that, but it lingered in the back of her mind, a sore place she avoided touching but always knew was there.

If anything, Jasper's failure to reply was worse. He had looked after her and told her to call him, and now, nothing.

To distract herself, she began to investigate the knowledge emergencies. However, even the assistance of two magical cats and the internet wasn't helping. Jemma reread what she had written in her notepad:

First known emergency: Charing Cross Library.
In attendance: Luke and me. Raphael was meant to go.
Particulars of book: appears to be a shifter book. Title: Ephemera From a Life of Transformation. She made a note to re-examine it when she next had a reason to go to the stockroom.

Behaviour of book: repulsion over a small area. Result: successful capture and storage in FB stockroom.

So much for that, but where had it come from? She found the number of Charing Cross Library and wrote it down. Hopefully she could sneak in a phone call the next day when Maddy was at lunch.

There was little to say about the next emergency.

London Library. Book reported as attracting other books. No other strange behaviour. Resolved easily by Lennox Nash. Details of capture: unknown. Current location of book: unknown. Title: unknown. Details of book: worn, maroon binding with gold lettering. Sounds very similar in appearance to first book.

And now for the most recent emergency. She looked into her mug. *Might make a fresh brew.* While in the kitchen, she also wiped the worktops, fetched a new tea towel, and put her shelf of cookbooks into alphabetical order by surname. Eventually she could find nothing else to do and returned to her seat.

Location: Maughan Library, Chancery Lane. Emergency reported by: unknown. Possibly first librarian. They were expecting Raphael; maybe he's visited them before.

Behaviour of book: ricocheting around library leaving soot and smoke, infecting other books. When invited, books launched at me.

She frowned. *Except I didn't invite them. I just asked the books what was wrong.* She laid down her pencil. If anything, the books had been having a tantrum, hitting out at the library and the person trying to help. They hadn't dared to attack the librarians, though – possibly because they might have been punished by being put into storage. That made her smile. *But the librarian said those books shouldn't even have been in the room...*

Type of book: Management and possibly self help. Result: books calmed down, more by luck than skill. One book escaped. Minor injuries sustained by Assistant Keeper. Some glass broken. Books appeared undamaged.

She sighed, and began a new line.

Wider result: police called. Several witnesses of phenomenon, including two librarians. Adverse publicity in local media.

At least Sergeant Hawkins hadn't contacted her. She wondered whether he was giving her a few days to clear her head, or whether her old phone was screening the call. Then again, surely he would have left a voicemail. *Maybe, just maybe, it's blown over.*

The next day, she used the pretext of finding more romance novels for the window display to go into the stockroom. Three Mills and Boons and a copy of *The Princess Bride* later, she approached the corporate finance section and drew out the silver key she had removed from her keyring earlier.

The box was cool, and when she opened it, the book was quiet. Cowed, almost. Perhaps it knew it could do her no harm, since she was not susceptible to its charms.

Jemma opened the book and riffled through it. It was as she had thought: five chapters on various expeditions as a werewolf, including the dangers and joys of such a metamorphosis, and a whole section on the advantages gained by transforming into an exact likeness of other people. Nothing so humble as a bat or a frog: the writer was aiming big. She couldn't discover how the author, who remained anonymous, had achieved this; they merely said that transformation was an ability they had cultivated over time, to the point where it was accomplished without pain in a few seconds. She could imagine how the book would have appealed to Raphael, and shuddered at what might have happened if he had gone to the library instead of her.

'Have you found them?' Maddy called.

Hastily, Jemma put the book away and came out with her selections. 'Sorry. Some books were mis-shelved.'

Maddy looked offended. 'I can assure you everything is where it should be. Anyway, I'm going for my lunch, if that's OK with you.' She picked up her bag.

'Fine by me,' said Jemma. 'Don't forget that I'm taking Luna to the vet at quarter past one.'

'I know,' said Maddy. 'That's why I'm going now.'

Jemma waited a few minutes before taking her phone from her bag and dialling. 'Hello, Charing Cross Library?' said a wary voice.

'Hello, could I speak to Rebecca, please?'

'Speaking. Who is this?'

'It's Jemma James, Assistant Keeper. I dealt with a knowledge emergency for you a few days ago, and I wondered if I could ask you some questions.'

A long pause. 'Yes, but not over the phone or in the library. I could meet you somewhere for lunch.'

'I'm sorry, I have to take my cat to the vet. Could we meet after work?'

'Yes, if you like. Can you do Caffè Teatro at 5.30?'

'I'll be there,' said Jemma. 'Thank you.'

'No, thank you. I need to talk to someone about this, and it's – difficult.' The call ended, and Jemma suspected another member of staff had come within earshot.

Luna and Folio walked in from the back room, jumped on the counter and sat down.

'I hope you'll come quietly,' Jemma said to Luna, remembering how good she had been when she visited the vet at her first check-up, following her unexpected arrival. 'I'm not taking both of you.'

Folio purred and rubbed his head against Luna, who

began to wash his face.

'I should put you two in our Valentine's display,' said Jemma. 'We might actually sell books.'

An hour later, she found herself regretting that comment. 'You're sure?'

'Absolutely sure,' said the vet. 'Luna is pregnant, and I expect her to deliver her litter in a few weeks' time. I don't think it'll be a big litter, as I assume this is her first time' – he looked severely at Jemma – 'but everything is in order and she's perfectly well.'

'That explains the eating,' Jemma murmured, more to herself than the vet. 'Should I bring Luna back when she's, um, ready? How will I know?'

The vet laughed. 'Luna probably won't need any help,' he said. 'Just in case, here's our out-of-hours number.'

Jemma visualised herself lying awake in the small hours of the night, one eye open for any sign of imminent labour.

'There's plenty of information on the internet,' said the vet. 'Don't worry.'

Luna got up and sauntered into her carrier. Jemma tried to decide whether she was walking any differently, but she couldn't spot anything. 'I thought she was too young,' she said. 'I didn't know she could get pregnant.'

'Ah, lots of people make that mistake,' said the vet. 'Cats aren't humans. And I hope that once she's delivered her litter, you'll consider making sure it doesn't happen again.'

'I'll think about it,' muttered Jemma, and picked up the carrier. She thought about it more seriously when she was confronted with the bill.

'Well, Luna,' she said as they walked down Charing Cross Road, 'I don't need to ask why Folio was looking so pleased with himself, or why you two have been so affectionate lately.' *At least someone's in a loving relationship*, she thought bitterly. Carl still hadn't rung her back.

Right on cue, her phone rang. Not her new phone, though. The old one. She dug it out of her bag; the display said *Lennox Nash*.

She considered declining the call: *I'm on my lunch hour.* But he'd know. He would have phoned the Friendly Bookshop first and spoken to Maddy. *I may as well get it over with.* She pressed *Answer*.

'I don't care if you're on your lunch,' Lennox shouted. 'I don't care if you're at the vet's with your cat. I don't even care if the vet has his hand up your cat's bottom. Get yourself to Burns Books right now!'

Jemma stopped dead in the middle of the street. 'What's happened?' she asked, and the dread which had shivered down her spine when she saw his name on her phone flooded through her until she shook.

'I said get here *now*!' And the phone went dead.

Chapter 16

At first Jemma thought a black cloud hung over the bookshop, as if its own personal thunderstorm might arrive shortly. Then she realised it was much, much, worse. The black cloud was a cloud of smoke, and it was growing.

A crowd had gathered outside the bookshop. Some were regular customers, some people she didn't know. Felicity and Jerome were staring at the bookshop, holding hands. She tapped Felicity on the shoulder. 'Has someone called the fire brigade? Is anybody in there?'

Felicity regarded her blankly. 'It isn't a fire. No one knows what it is. But it isn't good.'

Jemma felt the rumble rather than heard it. It was coming from beneath her feet. 'Woah,' cried the crowd, lurching as if they were on the deck of a ship in a storm.

Jemma tried to attract Felicity's attention but she was watching the bookshop intently, her mouth half open. Jemma pushed her way through the crowd, wrenched open the door of the bookshop, and went in.

The ground floor of the bookshop was empty. Anyone

still inside must be downstairs. 'Hello?' she called.

No response.

She moved into the back room and tried the door of the stockroom. It was locked, and the door handle was cool. *Whatever's going on must be downstairs.* Her knees trembled and she tightened her grip on the handle. 'Hello!' she shouted. Still no reply.

There was nothing for it; she would have to go downstairs, and the lift was out of the question. She descended carefully, holding on to the banister as the stairwell vibrated around her.

A wisp of pale smoke curled beneath the great oak door, and tears welled in Jemma's eyes. *It's come here. Whatever it is, it's come here.* She clenched her teeth and opened the door. A gust of warm, stale air blew in her face, and she blinked.

The first person she saw through the haze was Luke, clinging to a bookcase. She couldn't tell whether he was holding it to steady himself or to keep it from falling. Around him, bookcases strained and groaned as if they would split. 'Luke! What's happening?'

'We don't know!' he cried. 'Things were fine this morning—'

Lennox strode towards Jemma, scowling. 'What have you done this time?' he roared. He looked as if he might shake her, and she drew back.

'I haven't done anything,' she said. 'I got your call and came straight here.' She found she was still holding the cat carrier, and set it down.

'Maybe Luna can help,' called Luke. 'Open the carrier.

Folio's hiding, but maybe the cats can work together.'

Lennox whipped round. 'The cats? Don't be ridiculous. And I said I didn't want that cat in the shop.' He glared at the counter, behind which the tip of a ginger tail was visible.

'They've got powers,' said Luke. 'It's worth a try.'

Maddy's head popped up from the café counter. 'Maybe you should have another go, Dr Nash,' she said. 'I'm sure you can get things under control.'

'I thought the shop was under control,' he said grimly. 'That's why I agreed to take it on.' He walked slowly to the counter. 'When Raphael asked me to oversee things for a few months, he assured me it would be a piece of cake: a part-time job that wouldn't interfere with my other interests.' He gave Jemma a bitter look. 'How wrong he was. If I'd known his Assistant Keeper was a chaos magnet, I wouldn't have touched this with a bargepole.' He took off his suit jacket and draped it over the counter, then removed his cufflinks and put them in his breast pocket. 'I shall have to take severe measures to get things back to anything approaching normal.'

'What are you going to do?' asked Jemma. Her heart was thumping, her stomach was churning, and blood sang in her ears. She felt as if she might be sick, or possibly explode with tension.

'Something I've only had to do once before,' he replied curtly. 'What possessed you to order those books, anyway?'

Jemma stared at him. 'What books? I haven't ordered anything.'

'Don't lie to me; of course you have. It must have been you. I can't decide whether you're completely incompetent, or if that's a front you put on to make trouble.'

'I haven't ordered any books!' she shouted.

A book whistled past her ear and hit Lennox in the chest, then fell to the floor. *Principles Of Geometry*.

'What's that doing here?' Luke said, eyes wide. 'The maths books live upstairs.' He looked at Jemma and his eyebrows drew together. 'You didn't bring that down with you, did you?'

'Of course not,' said Jemma. 'Was it one of the books in the mystery order he's been shouting about?'

'No it was not, and you know it!' bawled Lennox. 'Don't play the innocent with me. Who else would order a whole box of employee management books addressed to me? Who else would deliver such a calculated insult, then claim innocence? I've worked with people I don't get on with, believe me, but I have never seen such barefaced cheek.' He flung up a hand to deflect another book, which plummeted to the floor with a flutter of pages. *London Maps, Ancient and Modern*.

'And I've never worked with someone who deliberately set up a situation to harm me!' Jemma yelled back. 'Sending me to a serious knowledge emergency while you swan off on a train to Reading? An emergency that you set up! And how dare you reprimand me afterwards? You've done nothing but throw your weight around since you got here, and you treat the shop as an amusing little diversion from all your other jobs. You're the worst manager I've ever met.' She gasped and doubled over as a book whacked her in the stomach, then fell to the ground. *Topography of London,* she read.

'I've had enough of this,' said Lennox, and started to roll up his shirt sleeves. He did it carefully, deliberately, as if preparing to conduct a surgical procedure.

'What are you doing?' Jemma demanded.

'Be quiet,' he snapped. 'If you don't want to see it, get out.' He raised an arm, and Jemma heard Folio yowl. Whatever was about to happen, he knew.

'Stop it!' she shouted. 'Don't do it!' She ran forward, grabbed his arm, and forced it down.

'Take your hands off me,' said Lennox. He spoke quietly, but his tone was cold and sharp as a rapier made of ice. His eyes glittered green. 'I won't tell you again.'

'Good,' said Jemma. 'I'm not letting go; I don't trust you an inch. If Raphael knew what you were really like he would never have put you in charge—'

Maddy screamed, and Jemma twisted round just as one of the huge chandeliers crashed to the floor. Another book hit her between the shoulder blades, and she squealed.

'Stop it!' she yelled, looking up. 'Please stop it!' She let go of Lennox's arm and raised her hands to the ceiling. Clouds of pale smoke almost obscured it, and the haze in the air was thickening. 'Please stop,' she pleaded, resisting the urge to cough. 'I am speaking to you as your manager, and as Assistant Keeper for Westminster. Whatever is wrong, we can fix it.'

'No you can't.' Lennox Nash stood, arms folded, sneering at her. 'You couldn't fix a loose button, Jemma.'

Silence fell, as if the shop were listening to them. Then

smoke billowed downwards and books slammed into shelves, counters, and people, until the air was full of dull slapping sounds.

'Everybody out!' cried Jemma, as best she could for coughing. She picked up Luna's carrier and stumbled towards the stairs as a bookshelf splintered apart. *'Run!'* She heard footsteps behind her as she ran upstairs, eyes streaming from the smoke, and beneath those footsteps, a strange percussion of thumps, groans, and splintering.

Jemma emerged onto the pavement, coughing, wheezing, gasping for breath. She put the cat carrier down and opened the door. After a couple of seconds Luna stepped out, meowing. She shook herself, sneezed, then began to wash. Folio ran over and butted her with his nose.

Jemma looked for the others. Luke had his arm around Maddy, who was weeping quietly. He was watching the shop, his face grave. Lennox, his face like stone, was rolling down his cuffs.

Jemma started. 'Where's Em? She isn't still inside, is she?'

She turned to go back into the shop, but Lennox moved forward and caught her arm. 'No, you fool, she went to the deli to pick up supplies.' He dropped her arm in disgust. Smoke billowed from the open shop door and he slammed it shut. 'Whatever it's doing, it can keep it to itself,' he said savagely. 'Godforsaken hole.'

Dark smoke seeped through the letterbox.

'Shut up,' said Jemma. 'The shop can hear you, you know. It hates you. It's always hated you.'

'Will you both be quiet?' Luke's voice rose to a wail.

'See what you're doing!'

Jemma, shocked out of her anger, looked at the door. The smoke was dark grey now, and the thumping within was audible. *He's right*, she thought. *It's my fault. I thought I could help, but I can't. I've made it worse, not better.* She burst into noisy tears, but no one came to comfort her. They were all staring at the bookshop.

Jemma's gaze followed theirs, and she gasped as the window burst outwards with a great rush of smoky air, and the pavement was covered in a shower of glass.

Chapter 17

Jemma waited nervously while the dust settled and the smoke dispersed. What would the bookshop do next? But no books flew out of the shop, and no more sounds of destruction came from within.

'I think it's over,' said Luke.

'This is far from over,' muttered Lennox. 'I shall contact Raphael and let him know what's been going on.' He glared at his staff. 'Give it ten minutes, then I expect you to start clearing up. And find someone to get that window boarded. You're going nowhere till the shop is secure.' He pulled his phone from his pocket and stalked off, angrily punching at it with his forefinger.

'What happened?' Em wheeled over a trolley laden with boxes. On top was a Rolando's brown paper bag, corners twisted. She looked from one to the other of them. 'What on earth happened?'

Jemma shrugged, and her hands fell to her sides. 'The shop got angry.'

'What was I thinking?' murmured Maddy. 'Such a

horrible man…'

Luke squeezed her gently. 'Don't worry, Maddy, he won't hurt you. I'll see to that.'

Maddy squirmed away from him. 'I can take care of myself, thank you,' she said. 'Are there cinnamon rolls in that bag, Em?'

'Yes.' Em untwisted the bag and held it out to her. 'If I'd known what was happening, I'd have got two bags. At least.'

They all took a cinnamon roll and munched while regarding the shop. The bookshelves on the upper floor were still standing, though some had moved slightly. Jemma winced at the thought of what might await them downstairs.

'Will the café be safe?' asked Em.

'No idea,' said Jemma. 'Whatever happens, we can't set the bookshop off again.' She remembered the hot sweet tea she had drunk at the Maughan Library, and her mouth watered.

'Where's Dr Nash?' asked Em.

'Sulking,' said Luke. 'Raging.' He looked at Maddy, but she kept her face averted. 'This is at least half his fault, anyway.' Jemma bit her lip and studied the shards of glass on the pavement.

'What did he do?' said Em.

'He's been keeping the shop under a spell since he got here,' said Luke. 'It was bound to revolt at some point, and that box of books was the final straw.' He walked over to Jemma. 'Jemma, be honest. Did you order those books?'

'No!' cried Jemma. 'Why would I do that? I've got

enough to do with running my own shop and dealing with the emergencies that keep happening. I haven't got time to play stupid tricks.'

Luke took a step back. 'Sorry. He just seemed so sure it was you. Anyway, we should see if it's safe to go in. The shop won't tidy itself.'

Em turned to the crowd, who were still gaping at the shop and muttering to each other. 'Show's over, everyone; we're going in to tidy up. Obviously the bookshop is closed until further notice. Thank you.'

Slowly, the crowd dispersed.

'Thanks,' Jemma murmured as they filed into the shop, the cats slinking between their legs. 'I don't have the words right now.'

'Oh, you had the words,' said Luke, with an exasperated look on his face. 'When I said that Dr Nash was at least half responsible, you didn't help.'

'I tried, but the shop wouldn't listen!' Jemma felt a sob rising in her throat, and swallowed it.

'That isn't what I meant,' said Luke, his voice serious. 'I reckon the shop would have calmed down if you and Dr Nash hadn't had a stand-up row downstairs.' He sighed. 'Can you three go and see how bad the damage is? I'll put the kettle on up here and ring a joiner about the window.'

Jemma, thoroughly rebuked, went downstairs with the others. At least the great oak door was intact, if smoke stained. She pushed it open, her heart in her mouth.

It wasn't actually as bad as she had feared. The chandelier still lay on the floor, and a couple of bookcases had collapsed into jagged pieces, but the books scattered over the floor appeared in good condition, and the smoke had gone.

'Good grief,' said Em, gazing at the scene. 'What on earth did you and Dr Nash say to each other?'

'I said he was the worst manager I'd ever had,' Jemma replied. 'Among other things.'

'Seems fair,' said Em. 'I didn't mind him too much, but he had his knife into you from the start.'

Maddy burst into tears. 'I hate him! He tricked me!'

Jemma led her to a chair and sat her down. 'What do you mean, he tricked you?'

Maddy raised a woebegone face. 'I don't know how he did it, but somehow all I could see was him. He was so clever, and sophisticated, and nice.' Jemma held her tongue, although she would have loved to comment. 'But when he argued with you just now, it was as if he'd taken that off, like a cloak, and he was no different from everybody else.'

'I sort of know what you mean,' said Jemma. 'When I first saw him he seemed really dashing. I kind of said "Wow" to myself. But then we disagreed over who to appoint and I decided I didn't like him.' She turned to Em. 'How about you?'

Em shrugged. 'One of those handsome men who have a way with them, I guess. Anyway, let's get as many books back on the shelves as we can, then see what else needs doing.'

As Jemma picked up books and shelved them, her suspicions were confirmed. Almost all the books were undamaged: the worst she could find was an occasional dog-ear which could have been there already. *So the shop didn't let go completely.* 'I'll check the stockroom,' she said. 'I should have done that first, but I think I'm still in shock.'

'I'm not surprised,' said Em. 'You're still recovering from that business at the other library. You probably shouldn't even be in work.' She grinned. 'While you're at it, see if you can hurry Luke along with that tea.'

Jemma unlocked the stockroom door and braced herself. When she opened it, though, everything seemed normal. The shelves were still stacked with boxes and the special books were still in their places, some restrained with silver chains.

On impulse, she pulled a box of books from the shelf and opened it. On top was *Trigonometry Explained*, under it a *London A-Z*, and beneath that, *Parishes and Wards of Greater London and the City*. 'This means something,' she murmured. 'But what?'

'Tea?' Luke passed her a steaming mug. 'Dr Nash would probably throw a fit if he saw us bringing drinks into the stockroom, but he isn't here.' He clinked mugs with her. 'Cheers.'

'I thought you'd want a stronger drink after that,' said Jemma.

He grimaced. 'I've gone off it lately. Not sure why. Maybe it's because I'm sad about Maddy.'

'She's seen through Dr Nash, anyway, and about time too.' They drank their tea, considering. 'What did you make of him?'

'He seemed OK at first,' said Luke. 'For thirty seconds or so. Then he gave me a look, and I knew he'd be trouble.'

'What sort of look?' said Jemma.

'The sort that says, "I know what you are".' Luke drank more tea. 'People don't usually spot me so quickly. I wondered if someone had told him. Maybe Raphael did. After all, it's useful information to have about one of your staff.' He snorted. 'He's far more dangerous than me, whatever *he* thinks.'

'Do you think so?' Jemma didn't doubt it, but she was keen to hear Luke's view.

'He's one of *those* guys. Always wants his own way, always sure he's right. I've met a few of those. A lot of the time he probably is right, but not always. And when he knows he's wrong, he can't take it. Hence the stomping off. I'd love to know where those books came from, though.'

'Is the box still around?' asked Jemma.

'It should be. I took it downstairs earlier. The delivery guy was adamant that Dr Nash had to sign for it, and he was holding forth to a customer.' He rolled his eyes.

'Let's go and see.' Jemma started for the stairs, but Luke remained where he was. 'Aren't you coming?'

'I'd best stay up here and make sure nobody tries to loot the shop. A joiner's coming in half an hour.' Jemma was fairly sure that Luke's reluctance to go downstairs was much more about Maddy than possible thieves, but kept that to herself.

'OK, what does the box look like?'

'Just a medium-sized cardboard box. No logos or anything, and the courier took the slip with him.' He thought. 'The guy had a green uniform, if that helps.'

'Maybe it will. I'll go on a box hunt.' On impulse, she gave Luke a quick hug. 'I'm sure things will work out.'

'Thanks.' Gently, he disengaged himself. 'Wish I was so sure.' He waved a hand at the kitchen area, where two more mugs waited on a tray. 'Take those, would you?'

'Can someone open the door?' Jemma called when she reached the bottom of the stairs. Usually she would manage the door herself, but she felt shaky.

Em let her in. 'All right upstairs?' She took a mug from the tray. 'There's probably another round of cinnamon rolls in the bag.'

'Cool.' Jemma delivered a mug to Maddy. 'Has anyone seen a cardboard box with management books in? The ones Dr Nash was shouting about?' The floor was mostly clear, apart from the pile of wood and paper that was the two ruined bookshelves and their contents. 'It can't have gone, can it?' She scanned the huge room for a plain cardboard box, then began to remove books from the wreckage of the two bookshelves. Five books in, she saw brown cardboard. 'Here it is.'

'Careful,' said Maddy. 'You should put on protective gear.'

Jemma had already cleared the books covering the box. 'It feels cool,' she said. 'I think it's all right.'

'For heaven's sake!' Maddy ran forward, took Jemma's arm and pulled her away. 'Look at what just happened! Do you want to get hurt?' She turned. 'Em, can you fetch an emergency kitbag from upstairs, please. I'd go, but I don't trust Jemma to behave herself.' She muttered something.

'What was that, Maddy?' said Jemma.

Maddy glared at her, eyes blazing. 'I said that Dr Nash isn't the only pigheaded person around here.'

'Oh. Sorry.'

A minute later, Em returned with the bag. Jemma pulled on a mask and gloves and stuck the book tongs into the waistband of her trousers. 'OK, I'm going in.' She eased open the flaps of the box. Nothing. No smoke, no sparks, no heat.

She took out first one book, then another, and laid them on the stone floor. They appeared to be perfectly normal books, very like the ones which had thrown themselves at her in the Maughan Library. Almost identical, in fact. She gasped, and got quickly to her feet.

'What is it?' Maddy and Em came to stand on either side of her, both staring at the box.

'I was wrong,' said Jemma. 'I thought Lennox set up the emergency at the Maughan Library to attack me, but I was wrong. The books weren't meant for me, because I wasn't supposed to go. They were meant for him.'

Chapter 18

'I've been such a fool,' Jemma said slowly. 'I should have realised I'm not the only manager here.'

'Well, hardly,' said Em.

'We must warn him.' Jemma got her phone and dialled Lennox's number, but the call went straight to voicemail. 'He's probably still on the phone to Raphael. Do you think he'll persuade Raphael to return?'

The others gazed at her hopefully, then Em shrugged. 'Would you return from Italy to take on a horrid situation in London in the middle of winter?'

'There is that,' said Jemma. 'And that first knowledge emergency was targeted at Raphael.' Em looked at her enquiringly. 'The shifter book.' She sighed. 'If we were in a fantasy novel, there'd be a plot twist about now. Raphael would never have left. He'd have been disguised as Lennox Nash all along, so that he could magically transform back into himself and save the day.' She studied the glum faces surrounding her. 'But I guess that won't happen.'

Luke came into the room. 'The joiner's here,' he said.

'Did you find the box, Jemma?'

'I did. From the look of things, that was the epicentre of the damage.' Jemma swallowed. 'I can see why Lennox felt got at. I think the emergency at the Maughan Library was directed at him, not me. The box delivered to the shop this morning was another attempt to target him, because the last one failed.' She clenched her fists. 'We have to find out who's behind this.'

Luke eyed Maddy. 'You're right; we must work together. If that's OK.'

There was a slight flush on Maddy's normally pale face. 'You can stay provided you don't do any – you know.'

'I won't. I promise.' Luke sat down at a large round café table.

'OK,' said Jemma, 'what do we know?' She joined him at the table and took out her notepad. 'I've made notes about the emergencies so far, but we need to add what's happened today. The shop is telling us something.'

'What makes you say that?' asked Em.

'Look around you,' Jemma replied. 'I thought it would be much worse, and the stockroom's untouched. *Geometry books*.' She scribbled in her pad.

'Excuse me?' said Em. 'I know you like your spreadsheets, but this is new.'

'Not me, the shop,' said Jemma, continuing to write. 'I opened a box in the stockroom. There was a book on trigonometry and one about London parishes.'

'And the book that hit Dr Nash was a maths book,' said Luke. 'It shouldn't have been down here.'

'The shop was trying to attract our attention,' said

Jemma. She bit her lip. 'We weren't listening, because we were too busy arguing.' She looked up at the ceiling, where the cord for the fallen chandelier hung limp. 'I'm really sorry.'

'The shop knows,' said Luke, putting a hand on her arm. 'What were the other books?'

'I suspect they've been tidied up,' said Jemma, 'but I definitely remember one on topography in London. And one of the books I took out in the stockroom was a London A-Z.'

'I'll go and find them,' said Luke, and got up.

'How will he know which ones they are?' asked Em, sitting down at the table.

'He won't need to search hard,' said Jemma. 'If the shop wants Luke to find a book, it will show the book to him.'

Luke returned with a box of books, which he put on the table and opened. 'Here's the *A-Z*,' he said, 'and the London parish book.'

Jemma glanced at her notepad. 'We could plot the location of each emergency on the map,' she said. 'Although I hate writing in books.'

Em went to the shop counter and returned with scissors and a pack of Post-its. 'We can cut little sticky squares.'

'Good thinking.' Jemma looked up the page for Charing Cross Library and stuck a small yellow square on it. 'That's one. And we've had an emergency here today.' She put another dot on the location of Burns Books. 'Now, Chancery Lane…' She riffled through the index and stuck another dot on. 'This isn't telling us much, though.' She made a mental note of the page numbers and consulted the small-scale map of London at the front. 'That makes a sort of flat triangle.'

'I can tell you something,' said Luke, holding up *Parishes and Wards of Greater London and the City*. 'I've just found a map in here. The Maughan Library is in Farringdon Without. It's in the City of London, but outside the old London Wall.'

'So it's sort of in and out of the city at the same time,' said Jemma. She could feel herself trembling. 'What does that mean, though?'

'Probably that it's time for lunch,' said Em. 'I don't know about you, but I'm starving, and it's well past three o'clock.' They followed her gaze to the café counter. 'Those paninis will go out of date today. I'll see if I can get the warmer going.' She got up and Maddy, after a glance at Luke, joined her.

'Maybe Burns Books is built on a ley line,' said Luke, paging through the book. 'That wouldn't surprise me one bit.'

Jemma moved her chair a little closer. 'Can I ask you a question?'

Luke looked at her for a long moment. 'Yeah, you can ask. Can't guarantee I'll answer, though.'

'When Maddy told you not to do anything just now, what did she mean?'

Luke folded a Post-it note in half, sticky side inwards, slipped it into the book and closed it. 'You're sure you want to know?'

Jemma held his gaze. 'Is it bad?'

'Depends on your point of view.' He leaned back in his chair and his pale-green eyes twinkled. The smile curving his lips broadened, and Jemma noticed he had two shirt buttons undone. A lock of black hair fell over his forehead, and he brushed it away slowly, gazing at her. 'That.'

'You promised you wouldn't, Luke!' Maddy yelled from the counter.

'It wasn't meant for you, Maddy.' Luke looked his normal self again, though a little tired. 'I was demonstrating to Jemma.'

'I think I see,' said Jemma. For an instant she had felt an impulse to touch Luke's hand, or his hair, maybe undo another button... She swallowed. 'You can just do that?'

'Yes,' said Luke. 'That was an extreme example, but it's useful in everyday life. Most vampires can do it. Cast glamour, that is.'

Cast glamour... Jemma stared at him, then reached into the box and found a dictionary. Buried at the bottom of the definition were the words *Archaic: enchantment, magic*, and a note that it derived from a Scots alteration of the word *grammar*. 'Every day's a school day,' she said. 'So is that what Lennox does? He's not a vampire, is he?'

'Not he,' said Luke. 'But that's how he sensed me. I was putting on a bit of front to meet the new boss, and he saw right through it, and me.' He leaned forward. 'That's why Maddy fell for him; she's quite susceptible.'

Jemma glanced at Maddy, who was putting paninis on plates. 'True: that's how Brian managed to control her.' She shivered. 'You must look after her, Luke.'

He shrugged. 'I'd like nothing better, but maybe that

ship has sailed.'

Maddy pushed the plates across the counter. 'Lunch is served,' she said, and turned back to the coffee machine.

'Give her time,' said Jemma. 'She's had an awful shock.'

'Haven't we all.' Luke stared moodily into the distance. For a second Jemma thought he was projecting glamour again, then decided he was just cross. She got up and walked to the counter. 'Is the tuna melt for me?'

'Yes,' said Em. 'Mozzarella, pesto and Parma ham for Luke. I figured he wouldn't mind the ham.'

'Tomato, basil, and black olives for me,' said Maddy.

'And a bacon and brie melt for me,' said Em. Jemma eyed her slim figure, and as always, wondered whether Em had hollow legs. Unless she had glamour-casting capabilities... She pushed the thought away, picked up her plate and Luke's, and took them to the table.

Em made fresh drinks and they sat munching companionably. It reminded Jemma of her university days, meeting friends at the library café – except that now the stakes were so much higher than a few marks on an essay.

They heard footsteps, and a man in a blue polo shirt stuck his head round the door. 'All boarded up. Who do I give the bill to?'

'That would be me,' said Jemma.

He came over and laid the piece of paper in the middle of the table. 'I'll see you out,' said Luke, getting up. 'You don't know any good glaziers, do you?'

The joiner tapped the side of his nose. 'I can give you some names. Might be booked up, though. Lot of bust windows around London at the moment.' Jemma waited until his back was turned, then made a quick note.

She finished her food and sat back, sipping her tea. *Why did Lennox's glamour fail to work on me so soon? Did he use it on Raphael? Was that how he got the job? Could he have influenced Raphael to go abroad in the first place?* Then she checked herself. *Stop it, Jemma; you're looking for reasons not to trust him. Given what you said to him earlier, he's got plenty of reasons not to trust you.*

Luke came downstairs with a sheet of paper in his hand. 'Got three names.'

'Can you ring and ask them to come and quote?' asked Jemma. 'I'll try phoning Dr Nash again.'

Luke's eyebrows drew together slightly, and he looked as if he were listening for a distant sound. 'No point,' he said. 'He's coming back.' Sure enough, two minutes later the shop bell jangled, footsteps descended the stairs, and Lennox Nash walked into the room.

Chapter 19

The first thing Jemma noticed was that Lennox wasn't striding, or stalking, but merely walking. He had his hands in his pockets, and an air of not being in a particular rush. The anger had left his face, too, and his expression was neutral. She wasn't sure whether that was an act.

'I see the window's boarded up,' he said. 'Thank you. I also note that this room is considerably tidier, but you will have to shift those broken bookcases.'

'I'll sort that out,' said Luke. 'We were busy assessing the damage and waiting for the joiner to finish.'

'Of course.' He eyed the empty plates on the table, but said nothing. 'You'll need to get that chandelier fixed, too. If we reopen tomorrow we can't have that wire hanging loose.'

Jemma studied him, trying to pinpoint what had changed. He didn't look any different, but it wasn't as if he'd had a supernatural glow in the first place. He seemed more relaxed, less tense. She remembered how Luke had seemed a little tired after casting glamour, and wondered how exhausted Lennox was at the end of a hard day being charismatic.

'Did you want to say something, Jemma?' Lennox enquired, and she jumped.

'No... Well, yes. I want to say that I'm sorry. I accused you of setting a trap for me, and I was wrong. The situation at the Maughan Library was a trap for you. I rang you, but your phone was engaged.'

'Yes, I expect it was,' said Lennox. 'I was speaking to Armand Dupont.'

'Oh.' *He went over Raphael's head.*

'I had intended to speak to Raphael, but he appears to be incommunicado.' The corner of his mouth twitched a fraction. 'In any case, the end result would be the same. You're still stuck with me, whatever you think of that.' He surveyed the room, taking in the bookshelves, the armchairs, the tables. His gaze lingered for a moment on Luna and Folio, who were curled up together in an armchair, but he remained silent.

'None of that matters,' said Jemma. 'We need your help, and you may still be in danger. Whoever's behind this has targeted you once, and they're bound to try again.'

He considered this. 'They'll have to do better than sending a box of books.' He shrugged. 'If I hadn't thought you'd sent them on purpose, I'd probably have put them on the shelves and sold them. The rest was the shop reacting to an argument, that's all. Anyway, you seem to have things in hand, so if you can arrange about that chandelier—'

'You can't leave!' cried Jemma. 'We need you.'

'I'm flattered.' It was probably the first genuine smile

she had seen from him.

'No, we really do.' She grabbed her notepad, went over to him, and explained their findings. He listened, but his expression didn't change.

'Mmm,' he said, when she had finished. 'Would you care to hear my opinion?'

Earlier that day Jemma would have turned him down flat, but now… 'Yes, I would.'

'Very well. I'm sorry to say it, but I think you're barking up the wrong tree. You found a pattern because you're looking for one, and you're fitting the pieces together to make it.' He sighed. 'You see a book on geometry, you see a shape, and you put them together. You see a manager, you see books about management, and you relate them to each other.' She would have felt less crushed if he had sounded angry or contemptuous, but his voice was matter-of-fact, as if correcting a student.

'It makes sense to me,' she said, and she heard the defensiveness in her voice. 'I know there are pieces missing.' She looked up at him. 'In fact, you can help us with one of those. When you went to the knowledge emergency at the London Library, which book was causing the trouble? And what happened to it?'

Lennox raised his eyebrows.

'You must remember,' said Jemma. 'Jasper Bantam didn't see the book up close, but he said you took it. A small, battered book with a red cover.'

'Oh yes,' said Lennox. 'I'd forgotten that.' He stood, thinking. 'Yes, Jasper showed me the trolley and it was fairly obvious that the book in the middle of the cluster was causing the problem. I pulled it out and popped it into the emergency kitbag for safekeeping, as it wasn't particularly volatile. Since I was going away for the weekend, I thought no more of it. I expect it's still in the bag; I'll go and see.' He strolled to the door.

Jemma and Luke exchanged glances. 'I still believe there's a pattern, even if he doesn't,' said Luke. 'What about you?'

'I don't know.'

'You were so sure before.'

And I was sure Lennox set me up. That was wrong, so maybe this is wrong too.

'Here we are,' said Lennox, coming back with the bag. 'I did mean to sort the book out, but, um…'

Jemma remembered what Raphael had said about him not liking paperwork. 'What's the book called? Is it to do with transformation?'

Lennox delved into the bag, and as he held up a small red volume, fear rippled through Jemma. He peered at the spine. 'No, it's called *Overconfidence And How To Combat It*.' He grimaced. 'Doesn't sound much fun. Want to see?'

'Er…' Jemma's heart thumped as if it wanted to escape. The roof of her mouth was dry, and she hastily drank some tea. 'I'm not sure.' She twisted the silver bracelet on her wrist. *Stop that, you'll break it.*

Lennox walked towards her, proffering the book. 'No, I don't want to see it,' she said.

'Sure?' He held the book out.

Jemma flung out her hand and he took a few rapid steps backwards, as if she had pushed him. 'There's no need to panic.' He put the book in his pocket, looking rather offended.

'Sorry, I… I don't know what happened.' The silver bracelet swung on Jemma's wrist, its beads gleaming. *So that's what it does*. She lowered her arm and clasped the bracelet with her other hand.

'No, neither do I.' Lennox glanced at the book, then back at her. 'That was quite a reaction. I assume you don't know the book?'

Jemma shook her head. 'I've never seen it before. I certainly haven't read it.'

'Well, since you don't like it, I'll chain it up and put it in the stockroom.' A thought struck him, and he held the book out to Luke. 'It doesn't bother you?'

Luke shook his head, watching the book. 'No, not at all.'

'Maddy, how about you?' He advanced, smiling.

Maddy got up so quickly that her chair fell backwards and ran to the café counter. 'Don't come near me!' She picked up the nearest thing – a tea strainer – and brandished it at him.

He laughed. 'It's only a book.' Then his expression changed. He put the book on a nearby table and moved towards Maddy again.

'Get away from me!' She dropped the tea strainer and opened a drawer, scrabbling for a more effective weapon.

Lennox threw up his hands and stepped back, looking confused. 'I'm probably tired,' he murmured. 'That will be it.' He picked up the book and walked to the door, glancing at them every so often. *I wonder…*, thought Jemma.

'Keep him away from me,' said Maddy, now holding a long sharp knife, 'or I won't answer for the consequences.'

'Maddy, we won't let him near you, but please calm down,' said Luke. He walked over to her and gently uncurled her fingers from the handle.

When Lennox returned, his face was serious. He stopped perhaps ten feet from the table. 'We've all done enough for one day. Never mind the chandelier. I'm going home, and I suggest you do too. Tomorrow is another day.' He left without looking back.

'That book was definitely a trap for you, Jemma,' said Em.

Jemma nodded. 'I don't know why I reacted like that. I had no control over it.' She turned the bracelet on her wrist. 'Someone knows my weakness. They know I worry that I'm not capable, and that I've blagged my way into this position, and they tried to exploit that.'

'Which proves your theory,' said Luke. 'Have you contacted your man at the London Library to see where the book came from?'

'Like Raphael, Jasper's incommunicado,' said Jemma, with a wry smile. 'Maybe he's avoiding me after I made him bring me home the other day.' Her cheeks warmed at the thought of it. 'So he's not *my* man at the library.'

'We could contact Rebecca,' said Luke. 'There must be someone who'll talk to us.'

'I nearly forgot!' Jemma exclaimed. 'I phoned Rebecca earlier and she asked to meet me at a café at half past five. She didn't want to talk in the library.'

'Would you mind if I came along?' asked Luke. Jemma

shot him a suspicious glance, but his demeanour was just as usual. 'I was there too, and I might remember something useful.'

'Good point. Anyone else coming?'

'No, thank you,' said Maddy, looking at Luke rather than her. Her expression was puzzled and slightly querulous, as if trying to work out what she thought of the situation.

'I'll pass,' said Em. 'In fact, I suggest Maddy and I stay here. I have a feeling that we may be required. Apart from anything else, there's still food to use up.' She giggled. 'We've already got a van. All we need is a Great Dane, and we can pretend we're in *Scooby Doo*.'

Luna rolled over, eyed Em from an upside-down position, and meowed.

'That's Luna's view on the Great Dane,' said Jemma. 'But yes, we're a team, cats included. We're a good team – a great team – and we'll work out what's going on and stop it.' She studied the earnest faces regarding her. 'We have to.'

Chapter 20

'If nothing else,' said Jemma, as she walked with Luke to Caffè Teatro, 'we may be able to pinpoint the colour of the courier's uniform.'

She, Em and Maddy had spent a frustrating half hour or so coaxing Luke's memory. 'You said the uniform was green,' Jemma had said. 'What sort of green?'

'I don't know. *Green* green.'

'Pale green or dark green?' asked Em.

Luke considered. 'Sort of in the middle.'

'OK. Was it bottle green? Pea green? Forest green? Apple green?'

Luke stared at her. 'The difference would be…?'

'Was it more a yellow green, or a blue green? Like teal, or turquoise?'

Luke shrugged. 'I'd probably know it if I saw it.'

Jemma fetched her laptop and found a colour chart. 'Here we go. Pick out the one closest to what you remember.'

Luke's finger hovered over the screen. 'That looks

right,' he said, pointing at a green that was almost but not quite bottle green. 'Although that one's familiar too,' he said, pointing at a colour that bordered on chartreuse.

'I give up,' said Jemma. 'No, I don't. Let's try this a different way.' She began to search for courier companies. 'It isn't any of the major ones,' she said, after a few minutes.

'This is so hard,' said Maddy. 'We don't know if it's a courier service, a service that book suppliers use, or just some man in green overalls pretending to be from a company.'

'True.' Jemma closed the laptop. 'Let's think about what we'll ask Rebecca.'

And now they were at the café. 'Before we go in,' said Jemma, 'are you planning to do that glamour thing on Rebecca?'

'I might,' said Luke. 'Are you asking me not to?'

'If you're doing it to get information, fair enough,' said Jemma. 'Not if you're going to flirt with her.'

'Me? Flirt?' said Luke. She wasn't sure if he was joking or not.

'Well, keep it down. We don't want half the café getting interested.'

Rebecca was sitting in a booth at the back of the café, a full cup of milky coffee in front of her. She had already seen them. Jemma suspected she had been waiting some time. 'Hi,' she said. 'I didn't know that – that you weren't coming alone.'

'I thought that as Luke was at the library too that day, he might be useful,' Jemma said casually. 'Is that all right?'

Rebecca's gaze shifted to Luke, who pushed his hair back from his forehead. 'I'm mostly here to learn,' he said. 'I'm very much the junior partner.'

'Oh, well in that case…' She managed a nervous smile. 'It feels odd that I'm talking to someone else about it. As if I'm being disloyal to the library. But that's silly, isn't it?'

Jemma slid into the booth opposite her and Luke followed suit. 'If you're worried – and you sounded as if you were when we spoke on the phone – it makes sense to discuss it.'

'Yes.' Rebecca sipped her coffee and made a face.

The waitress came over and they ordered a cappuccino for Jemma and a black decaf coffee for Luke. 'That's a strange combination,' said Rebecca. 'Black decaf coffee?'

Luke smiled. 'Too much caffeine affects my sleep.'

Rebecca studied her cup, her cheeks already turning a delicate pink.

'Let's begin,' said Jemma. 'When we came to the library, the book was shelved among the chapter books in the children's section. What can you tell us about how it got there?'

Rebecca gazed at her, doubt in her eyes. 'It was a normal morning at the library. Debbie, one of the assistants, was processing returns at the desk, and I was working through emails. When I looked up, a man was standing at the desk. He was in a green cap and overalls, and he had a book-shaped package in his hand. "Can you sign for this, please?" he said. Of course I did, and off he went.'

'Could you describe him?' asked Jemma. 'His appearance, the colour of his overalls, any logos?'

'Just a typical courier,' said Rebecca. 'I didn't recognise the uniform, and I didn't see any logos. I don't think there were any on the form I signed, either.'

'Can you remember the colour of the overalls?' Jemma persisted.

'They were a dark blue-green, like a forest of blue spruce trees. I remember thinking it would be a nice colour for a room.'

'Great.' Jemma couldn't resist a glance at Luke. 'What happened then?'

The drinks arrived, and Jemma tried not to fidget while cups were placed and pleasantries exchanged. Finally the waitress departed, and she turned back to Rebecca. 'Did you open the package?'

'No, I didn't open it. It was addressed to the library, not me, so I left it to Debbie. I had papers and a big report to read for a meeting that afternoon, so I was pushed for time. Then Debbie showed me the book and said she wasn't sure what to do with it. I hadn't ordered it, and there was no note, or a return address.' She took another sip of her drink.

'I looked the book up on the computer and it popped up in interlibrary loans. However, there was no record of which library the book had been sent from, and when I checked which of our members had requested it, the record that came up was blank. No name, and a birthdate of the first of January, 1900. I assumed it was a computer error, and told Debbie to shelve the book. I figured that if someone did come in for it, at least we would be able to find it.'

She paused, thinking. 'Debbie found the classification number, put the book on the trolley with the other returns, and shelved them all. Then it got busy. The next thing I knew, people were coming out of the children's library saying that they felt funny, and I found that book at the centre of it. I did ask Debbie why she'd put it there, and Debbie replied that that was what the computer said. So I phoned Raphael, and the rest you know.'

'Is there anything else you'd like to tell us, Rebecca?' asked Jemma.

Rebecca sipped her coffee cautiously, then toyed with her spoon. 'I don't think so. Now that I'm telling you about it, it seems silly. A sort of collective hallucination with no basis in reality.'

'We experienced it too,' said Jemma.

'If it was a collective hallucination then you would, wouldn't you?' Rebecca's voice had a hard edge.

Luke set down his cup and leaned forward. 'How do you feel when you're in the library, Rebecca? May I call you Rebecca?'

'Yes, of course.' Rebecca fiddled with the silver chain at her throat. 'I – well, it's a library, isn't it? The same as it always was.'

'Is it, Rebecca?' He laid his hand on the table and Rebecca glanced at it, then him. 'Is it just the same?' His voice was low, confiding.

'No.' The chain twisted in her hand. 'It doesn't feel the same,' she muttered. 'I don't like being alone there. I hold the keys, and that never used to bother me, but now when I open up I see movements in the shadows, and at night I hear whispering when I switch off the lights. It's as if something is living in the library: something I can't see. I mentioned it to Debbie once and she looked at me as if I'd gone mad. And my eczema's flared up.' She pushed up her sleeve and revealed a scaly, red patch of skin on her arm. 'It hasn't been this bad for years.' She let her sleeve fall. 'Maybe I'm overworking. Maybe I'm imagining things—'

'I don't think you are,' said Jemma.

'Neither do I,' Luke added. Rebecca beamed at him, and Jemma fumed inwardly that he was getting all the credit. Then again, Luke had charmed her into opening up.

'Even if I'm not,' said Rebecca, 'what do we do?'

'That's a good question,' said Jemma, 'and not one I can answer yet. I need to do some research, and possibly speak with my boss.' She felt a pang of dismay when she realised she had been thinking of Lennox, not Raphael. 'What I'd suggest is that you ring in sick tomorrow; that gives us time to investigate. Your assistant doesn't seem to be affected by what happened, and I'm sure she can hold the fort.'

Rebecca looked as if a weight had been lifted from her shoulders. 'Thank you. I didn't expect you to take me seriously.'

'Strange things have been happening lately,' said Jemma. 'This may be connected, but until we've investigated further we won't know for sure.' She finished her cappuccino. 'If you can let me have a personal number or email, I'll be in touch. We may want to return to the library.'

'Will you come too?' Rebecca asked Luke.

'That depends on my boss. But yes, probably.'

She gave him a shy smile. 'That would be nice.' She took out a pen, scribbled a phone number on a napkin, and pushed it across to Jemma, keeping her eyes on him.

'Right, we'd better be on our way,' Jemma said briskly. 'Thank you for all your help, Rebecca.' She rose. 'Come along, Luke, things to do.'

'Did I do something wrong?' Luke asked, as he strode down Charing Cross Road beside Jemma. She still found it annoying that he could keep up with her so easily.

Jemma stopped dead. 'There is such a thing as overdoing it, Luke. You practically had her eating out of your hand.'

'Sorry. It's just, you know, someone being nice to me for a change.' He looked woebegone. 'I miss Maddy.'

'Coming on to another woman isn't the best way to express that,' said Jemma.

'I wasn't, I was encouraging her to open up—'

Jemma sighed, and began walking. 'Maybe you were. But Rebecca is so susceptible to you that she makes Maddy look like Fort Knox.'

'I suppose.' They walked for a while in silence. 'What do you reckon about what Rebecca said?'

'I'm sure she's speaking the truth, and it's certainly interesting. We have a colour for the uniform, which will help, and we know how they got the book into the library.' Jemma frowned. 'It's a roundabout way to do it, though. Someone could just have come in wearing ordinary clothes and planted the book...' She took her phone from her bag. 'I'll try Jasper.' As usual, she couldn't get through. 'Still avoiding me,' she said, with a false lightness in her voice.

'Unless he isn't,' said Luke.

'Oh, I know why he's screening my calls,' said Jemma. Then she stopped again. 'Unless... The book wasn't meant for Rebecca, but it still affected her. The book wasn't meant for Jasper, but it may have affected him.'

'And it could be worse,' said Luke. 'Bigger library, bigger target.'

'The Maughan Library is bigger still,' said Jemma. 'I must find out what happened there after the incident, but I don't think they'll ever let me return.'

'Where does the attack on Burns Books fit in?'

'That wasn't planned in the same way,' said Jemma. 'That was another attempt to target Lennox. The books which arrived in the library would already have done whatever they needed to.' She paused. 'But what if this isn't over? Where would they strike next?'

'Somewhere bigger than the Maughan Library, I'd guess,' said Luke.

Jemma stumbled, and he caught her arm. 'Are you OK?'

'Somewhere bigger than the Maughan Library,' she replied, gazing up at him. 'One of the biggest libraries in the world, and it's practically on the doorstep.' Bile rose in her throat, and she swallowed. 'The British Library. That's what they'll go for.' She broke into a run. 'I just hope we aren't too late.'

Chapter 21

'Jemma, wait!' Luke caught up with her. 'What are we going to do?'

'I'm not entirely sure,' Jemma gasped, 'but we have to do something. We have to stop them. Or if the book is already there, we must find it and get it out.' She opened the door of Burns Books and they half fell in.

Em and Maddy were upstairs, waiting. 'What did you find out?' asked Maddy, looking at the pair of them. 'Tell us.'

'This isn't just about getting at Raphael, or me, or Lennox,' said Jemma. 'It's worse. The books are causing trouble wherever they're left. I bet that book Lennox brought back from the London Library was doing the same here, and affecting me.' She remembered how she hadn't been able to do a thing right, and how she had failed to calm the bookshop. 'At least that's safely chained up now, but there's a pattern. The venues are getting bigger, and we think they'll target the British Library next.'

'Oh no,' murmured Maddy. 'At least it's closed now.

That gives us time to come up with a plan.'

'It isn't.' Luke looked up from his phone. 'The library is open until eight tonight, and it's just gone six.'

'OK,' said Jemma. She went to the counter and fetched the two knowledge emergency kitbags. 'Luke, can you make sure these are complete. Em, can you search online for a courier or a delivery company with a dark blue-green uniform. Like a dark turquoise. I reckon their vans and their logo may be the same colour.'

'OK.' Em pulled out her phone. 'I can't think of any company that uses those colours, but it's worth a go.'

'What shall I do?' asked Maddy.

'Umm... Can you get the *A-Z* and add a dot for the British Library? It will make a triangle, of course, but I wonder what's inside that triangle.' Maddy scurried off. 'I'll phone Lennox, tell him what we've discovered, and get him to come with us. I hope.' Jemma grabbed her phone and went through to the back room.

The call went straight to voicemail. 'I'm afraid I can't come to the phone at present,' Lennox said smoothly. 'If you could leave a short message, I'll respond as soon as I can. Thank you so much for calling.'

The beep sounded. 'Lennox, it's Jemma. We think the books from the knowledge emergencies are causing after-effects. We're not sure how serious, but the libraries are getting bigger. We think they'll try the British Library next, so we're going there now. Please come and help. Call me.'

She ended the call and ran a hand through her hair. 'Why is it down to me?' she said, out loud.

'Because you're here.' For a moment Jemma thought it was her pesky inner voice talking, but then she saw Luke in the doorway. He held up the two kitbags. 'All present and correct. Anyway, it isn't just you. We're all going. We're not letting you face whatever this is alone.'

'Thank you,' said Jemma. 'Would you mind seeing what's left in the café? We can eat on the way.'

'Sure.' He made his way downstairs.

Jemma heard light footsteps running up. 'I did it,' gasped Maddy. 'Look.' She thrust the *A-Z* under Jemma's nose and Jemma saw a tall triangle with a narrow point at the top.

'Thanks.' She took the *A-Z* and, keeping a finger in the London map, consulted the pages that made up the area of the triangle. 'Oh heck,' she said, after a minute or two.

'What is it?' asked Maddy.

Luke appeared, carrying a bulging Burns Books paper bag. 'What have you found, Jemma?'

'If they are going to the British Library…' Jemma sketched the triangle with her finger. 'That area includes the British Museum, Sir John Soane's Museum, and lots of other libraries and bookshops. Including ours. If they get a hold on all that… I don't want to think about it. We'd better go.'

'I'll head outside and hold a taxi,' said Luke.

'No need.' Jemma went through to the main shop, took a Pencil of Truth from the drawer and grabbed a set of keys from their hook. 'We'll take Gertrude.'

***

'Jemma, please slow down,' pleaded Em. 'Does anyone

have an empty bag?'

'It's not me, it's Gertrude,' said Jemma. 'I'm sorry, but we'll be there soon.'

'I'm not sure if that's a relief or not,' Em muttered.

'Did you find any likely delivery companies, Em?' Jemma hoped the question would distract Em. She had set Gertrude to self-drive. They were certainly making much better progress than she had expected, given London traffic, but they were doing it by taking every shortcut, alley, back street, and convoluted diversion.

'I think so,' said Em. 'I found a company called River Logistics with a dark-turquoise livery.'

She held the phone out to Luke, who nodded. 'That's the sort of thing the delivery guy was wearing.'

'Great,' said Jemma. 'Show Maddy, and I'll look when we've stopped moving. We need to be able to spot them.'

'Any message from Dr Nash?' asked Luke.

Jemma shook her head. 'I took my phone off silent specially.'

'What did you expect,' said Maddy, wrinkling her nose. 'He's nothing but a – wooooaaahh!' She clung on as the van took a sharp bend, possibly on one wheel.

'Hopefully he'll make it,' said Jemma. 'I was thinking. If you wanted to plant a book that would have an effect on its surroundings in a library, when would you do it?'

'Just before it closed,' said Luke. 'That way there'd be less chance of anyone spotting it, and it could do whatever it was doing overnight.'

'Exactly,' said Jemma. 'So assuming that we don't find devastation at the library, they'll deliver the book near closing time.'

'In that case,' said Em, grimacing, 'would you mind telling this van to slow down?'

Gertrude screeched to a halt at the traffic lights outside the library, which were conveniently on red. Indeed, it was the first red light Jemma had ever encountered in the camper van.

'We can't park here!' cried Em. 'In case you haven't noticed, there are red lines on the road.'

'Fair point.' Jemma checked the rear-view mirror, but a line of traffic was forming behind them. 'Em, can you stay with Gertrude and get her parked somewhere nearby, please?'

'Why me?' said Em. 'I've never been in this van without feeling sick.'

'You can drive,' said Jemma. 'Not that you'll need to. Maybe you and Gertrude can get to know each other.' She scrambled out of the van, and Maddy and Luke followed suit.

'I don't believe this,' she heard Em murmur as she closed the driver's-side door.

They crossed the squares of the quiet, dark piazza, Jemma and Luke carrying the emergency kits. 'It seems all right,' she said, unconvinced, gazing at the huge orange-and-grey building. No smoke was visible, and no one was rushing out.

'Quick question,' said Luke. 'How do we get these bags through security? They won't like book-sized, lead-lined boxes.'

'I don't know.' A chill spread through Jemma. Had they

come so far, only to fail at this last, stupid hurdle?

A clear, piercing whistle made them turn. Lennox Nash was striding towards them, overcoat billowing. Jemma had rarely been so pleased to see anyone. 'You're earlier than I anticipated,' he said.

'We took Gertrude,' Jemma replied.

'That explains it. Let's get into the library, then you can fill me in on the details.' He took Jemma's bag and slung it over his shoulder. 'You two, stay with me. Maddy, I'll ask you to keep a few steps back. Nothing personal.'

Maddy made a face, but dropped back.

They walked into the huge, light building. Jemma gazed about her in an attempt to hold her nerve. *There's the shop, and the stairs, and the central gallery...*

'Dr Nash!' exclaimed the woman on bag duty in the entrance hall. 'I haven't seen you for ever so long. Have you been away?'

'I have,' said Lennox, beaming at her. 'I hope you don't mind, but I've brought a study group with me.'

'Oh no, not at all,' she replied, but Lennox was still moving forward, his bag unchecked. Jemma expected them to be called back at any moment, but kept going. She heard a sharp 'Excuse me,' and turned to see the woman beckoning Maddy over.

Maddy looked thoroughly mutinous while her bag was searched, but eventually the woman let her go and she rejoined them. 'Thanks for nothing,' she muttered, glancing at Lennox.

'Sorry, Maddy,' he replied, not in the least bothered. 'A necessary evil. Now, tell me what's been happening.'

As briefly as she could, Jemma gave him the gist of the evening's events.

His expression became grim. 'If you're right, that's pretty crafty. So we're watching for a delivery person, then.' He surveyed the huge space.

'Unless they've already done the deed,' said Jemma. 'I thought they'd wait till the last minute, to give the book its best chance of working.'

'That makes sense,' said Lennox. 'Though we don't know to whom the package will be addressed. The chief executive, I suppose, or the chief librarian.'

'Or maybe to the library,' Jemma replied. 'That way, the book will probably be left for someone else to deal with tomorr—'

The word caught in her throat as a man in a dark-turquoise uniform came into the library, carrying a medium-sized box.

Chapter 22

The courier turned left and went into the shop.

'I'll see what he's up to,' said Lennox. He strolled towards the shop.

Five minutes later, he came out. 'False alarm, I'm afraid: it was a box of pens. I did pick up a nice notebook, though.' He took it from his pocket and held it up.

'I'm very pleased for you,' said Jemma, 'but do keep your mind on the job.'

'A notebook is part of one's equipment,' he replied, drawing himself up.

The minutes ticked by. Jemma wondered whether one of the staff would come over and ask why they were loitering, but they were left alone. Occasionally people who were leaving eyed them, as if to say *Aren't you going to see anything while you're here?* However, no one approached.

'There aren't any other entrances, are there?' asked Maddy, glancing around as if a door might materialise out of thin air.

'There's another exit somewhere, I'm sure,' said Lennox. 'However, from what you've said, these people use the front door. It would be terribly unsporting of them to change their modus operandi at this point.'

'I doubt they're worried about being sporting,' said Jemma. Out of the corner of her eye she saw another courier enter the building, carrying a box. He walked past them, went up the short flight of stairs beside the box office, and kept going.

'I'll follow him,' said Jemma. 'I'll call you if I need help.' Luke handed her his kitbag and she set off.

She kept a few metres behind the courier. He was a middle-aged, wiry man, whistling a tune she didn't know. He didn't have the air of someone on an important mission, and she allowed herself to relax a little.

Her intuition was confirmed when he went to the café at the back of the building and handed the box to an assistant. She used a pair of scissors to cut it open, and withdrew packets of paper napkins. Jemma exhaled, and went back to the others.

'Napkins,' she said, letting the kitbag fall at her feet. 'They're playing with us.'

'Maybe they are,' said Lennox. 'But we don't let it get to us. We stay calm.'

'We are in the right place, aren't we?' said Jemma. 'I mean, it's the logical next step and it makes sense, but what if they're doing all this to keep us busy while they plant a book somewhere else?'

'It's a possibility,' admitted Lennox. 'Then again, if they think we have an inkling of their plans, they'll want to hit their target quickly. This River Logistics may well be a legitimate firm with no knowledge of what's going on. Indeed, that would make the most sense. The last thing the perpetrator would want is for their agents to appear nervous or apprehensive.'

After a few more minutes, Jemma checked the time. Almost seven thirty. 'They haven't got long now.' She tried her best to keep her voice level.

'Maybe they aren't coming tonight,' said Luke.

'They don't know we're on to them,' added Maddy. 'They probably think they've got weeks to make their arrangements.'

'They've moved pretty quickly so far,' said Jemma, her eyes still on the main entrance. More and more people were leaving now, some stopping before the entrance for a final chat, which made it harder to see what was going on.

Another courier in dark turquoise came through the door, moving smartly and wheeling three boxes on a trolley.

'I'll take this one,' said Lennox, and drifted after him.

'They're heading for the lift,' said Luke. He turned back to Jemma. 'I hope Dr Nash will be OK. Should I follow them?'

'I don't know,' said Jemma. 'Maybe—'

Another delivery man entered and passed them, making for the bookshop.

'I'll follow him,' said Luke, picking up the kitbag.

More minutes passed, and more people dispersed. The skin on the back of Jemma's neck prickled. *What's taking Luke so long? Surely they've delivered the box and someone has opened it. That would have happened at either of our bookshops. And where's Lennox?* She pondered. *Perhaps they've gone to one of the reading rooms.* She tried to recall how many there were. *That's odd: I thought I knew. I was here less than a month ago.*

She turned to ask Maddy if she knew how many reading rooms the library had, but Maddy was following yet another courier carrying a small padded envelope.

How ridiculous this is. We're chasing couriers round a library, and there are probably thousands of them in London. She giggled at the thought of hundreds of Jemmas and Lukes and Maddys and even Lennoxes, running round a maze of streets, pursuing fast-moving turquoise dots as if they were in a video game. *We should all go home and get a good night's sleep.*

She felt a dull sensation in the pit of her stomach. *I'm hungry, and Luke left the food bag with Gertrude. Em's probably working her way through it right now.* Then the feeling strengthened, and she realised it was not hunger, but nausea. She swallowed, and tasted copper in her mouth.

A young woman passed her. She had reddish-pink hair in two short plaits, and wore multicoloured leggings and big boots beneath her army-surplus coat. Somehow it suited her, and Jemma felt a pang of jealousy. *I'd look so stupid if I dressed like that.*

The woman walked away, a little rucksack jiggling on her back, and Jemma's queasiness was replaced by fascination. The woman was heading for the exhibition gallery on the left-hand side: Treasures of the British

Library. *I wonder what she's come to see. I didn't visit the exhibition last time I came. Maybe there's something new...* No more couriers had appeared, so she followed the woman into the gallery.

The room was dark, to preserve the exhibits, and a few people roamed about. Jemma wandered from case to case, taking little in. Indeed, she was struggling to remember what she had seen before. Her stomach rumbled and the coppery taste grew stronger, making her want to retch. *I should eat*, she thought. *Or would that make it worse?*

The woman with the plaits was heading for the small room on the right-hand side of the gallery, and Jemma followed. Suddenly her legs gave way, and she had to clutch a display case to keep herself upright. An elderly man glared at her. 'Sorry,' she whispered. Her eyes were watering as if she had walked into smoke. *What's wrong with me?*

The truth hit her like a freezing wave. *There's nothing wrong with me. It's her. And I have to stop her.*

She reached for the strap of the knowledge emergency bag, but it wasn't on her shoulder. Lennox had one bag, Luke the other. Jemma gazed at the bracelet twinkling on her left wrist, then rummaged in her bag, found the Pencil of Truth, and gripped it in her right hand. *This will have to do.*

Teeth gritted, she advanced on the little room. Her mind felt as if it had been packed in cotton wool...

As if Drusilla's playing mind games with me again.

Jemma stumbled towards the entrance, fighting the urge to vomit. The young woman was looking at an exhibit and unbuckling her little bag. She drew out a small black book —

'Stop it!' shouted Jemma.

The woman turned, eyebrows raised. 'I was only going to make a quick sketch,' she said.

'Let me see that book,' said Jemma, lurching forward.

The woman put it behind her back. Her puzzlement had become a frown. 'My drawings are no business of yours. Who are you, anyway, and why are you following me? I saw you staring at me when I passed you by the entrance.'

Jemma could hear people muttering outside. Her eyes were watering so much that she had to wipe them.

'She went this way,' someone said, and the elderly man entered with a security guard.

'May I ask what's going on?' the guard asked, looking from Jemma to the young woman and back.

'This woman was staggering about in the main room,' said the elderly man, indicating Jemma. 'And she's bothering this young lady.'

'Is that right?' the guard asked the young woman, who now appeared very demure.

'She followed me in here and tried to grab my sketchbook.' The woman held up the small black book. 'I don't think my sketches are all that interesting. And I've never seen her before in my life.'

'Madam, come with me, please.' The guard made to take Jemma's arm, but she dodged. 'Madam, please moderate your behaviour, or I shall call for backup.' He took a step forward and removed the walkie-talkie from his belt.

Jemma stared at him, dazed. Then she turned to the young woman, who was regarding her with a mocking smile she knew only too well.

Please don't let me be wrong. She leapt forward, grabbed the woman's wrist, and pressed the point of the Pencil of Truth into the back of her hand.

The woman cried out, and the book fell to the floor.

'Well, that's absolutely disgraceful!' cried the elderly man, but Jemma held on, waves of nausea rising in her throat. The slim wrist in her grasp grew hot and the skin blistered, while a dark-purple bruise spread from the point of the Pencil of Truth. She raised her eyes to the woman's agonised face and watched as the reddish-pink hair rippled into expensive highlighted blonde, the brown eyes lightened to hazel, and the pretty features hardened into the haughty lines that marked the face of Drusilla Davenport.

The security guard took a step back. 'What the—'

Jemma's nostrils flared and she almost vomited as an awful smell rose from the floor. The book was belching stinking fumes, and the floor beneath it was blackening.

'Decision time, Jemma James,' Drusilla muttered through clenched teeth. 'You can either keep hold of me, or capture that book. You can't do both.' She glanced over Jemma's shoulder. 'Oops, here comes the cavalry.' As Jemma half turned, Drusilla twisted from her grip and bolted from the room. As she ran, her hair became pink again.

'What's going on?' Luke appeared, followed by Lennox. 'Why did that woman run out of the library? And what's that horrible smell?'

'That woman was Drusilla,' said Jemma, and both their mouths fell open. 'First things first. Luke, give me your kit. We need to restrain this book before it destroys the library.'

Chapter 23

Jemma moved around the Friendly Bookshop, replenishing the shelves, while Maddy was at lunch. They had had plenty of customers that morning, perhaps making up for the time when the shop had been closed, but a busy morning in the bookshop was nothing compared to the activities of the previous evening.

It had taken Jemma and Lennox some minutes to get the small black book into a box and chain it. 'Don't touch that,' Lennox muttered, eyeing the book with distaste. 'Put gloves on, at least.'

Jemma obeyed and reached for the book, but the heat went straight through the gloves. 'Ow!' She snatched her hand back. 'Pass me the tongs. Unless you want to do it.' She looked up at Lennox.

He shook his head. 'You're closer.'

'Thanks.' Maddy, who had entered the room moments before, rolled her eyes at Jemma behind Lennox's back.

'What's going on?' asked the security guard, peering through the smoke.

Lennox smiled at him. 'Judging from the smoke and fumes, that book has been soaked in a chemical which is reacting with the floor.'

'Oh,' said the guard, stepping back.

'Nasty, isn't it?' Lennox continued. 'Best that we get it out of here, pronto.'

'May I ask who you are?' enquired the elderly man, looking extremely suspicious.

Lennox transferred the smile to him, then leaned forward confidentially. 'I'm not carrying full ID, as technically we're both off duty.' He took a card from his wallet and flashed it at the man, whose eyes widened. 'I don't think I need to say more.'

'No sir, indeed,' the man replied. If he had been wearing a cap, Jemma suspected he would have touched it.

'Gotcha.' Using both pairs of tongs, she executed a pincer movement on the book, which jerked in her grasp. 'Get a box and a chain ready.'

Luke delved into the bag, opened a lead-lined box, and held it at arm's-length. 'Don't let it touch me.'

'I'm doing my best.'

With an effort, Jemma pushed the book into the box and Luke slammed it shut. Lennox quickly passed a silver chain around the box, put the padlock through, and snapped it together.

The box shook, and a wisp of black smoke seeped from its edge. 'Like that, is it?' Lennox rummaged in the bag and brought out a bigger box. 'Pop it in there.'

Jemma put the box inside, and he chained it. This time, there was no movement. 'I think we've contained it,' he said, and everyone in the room breathed a sigh of relief.

'So is this chemical warfare?' asked the security guard. His tone suggested he knew about such things, but his eyes were very round.

'It's possible,' said Lennox. 'Until we've had a chance to analyse this book, I suggest you get everyone out of here. You don't know what's on that floor. Could be poisonous.'

The security guard checked his watch. 'It's nearly chucking-out time, anyway.' He motioned the elderly man out of the small room, then followed him into the main gallery. 'Everybody, there has been a minor incident and we are closing this gallery for cleaning. Please make your way to the main entrance. Thank you.'

He patrolled the room till everyone had left, speaking into his walkie-talkie at intervals, then returned. 'Do you need anything, sir? An escort, perhaps?'

'We'll be fine,' Lennox assured him. 'We have transport waiting.'

Jemma pulled off the gloves and examined her right hand. Her fingertips were red and sore. 'I should put my hand under a cold tap,' she said. 'If I hadn't worn these...' The room spun.

Lennox sprang forward and led her to a chair. 'Put your head between your knees. You've had quite an experience.'

Jemma breathed slowly and deeply, and the room stopped moving. She looked up at Lennox. 'What if Drusilla returns? Luke said she left the library, but she could have come back. She could have shifted into another identity.' She remembered the book at Charing Cross

Library, and the author's description of the pleasure they derived from assuming a different identity. 'She could be anyone.'

'Jemma, listen,' said Lennox. 'When Drusilla passed us she was clearly in pain; her arm looked burnt. You obviously did something to her, apart from making her assume her real form. She won't try anything like that again for some time.'

'But we don't know that,' said Jemma. 'Did you feel anything when she ran past you?'

'Yes,' said Luke, 'I felt ill.'

'So did I,' said Lennox. 'That means we have a good chance of spotting Drusilla if she reappears, whatever form she is in.'

'We should organise a rota,' said Jemma. 'We need someone here all the time to watch for Drusilla.' She pushed her hair out of her eyes and realised she was sweating. 'We must mobilise the whole Keepers' Guild to fight this.'

'You may be right,' said Lennox. 'But not tonight.'

'Yes, tonight! What if she comes back tomorrow morning and we're not ready?'

Lennox sighed. 'Very well. But let's talk it over first.' He smiled. 'Apart from anything else, you must be hungry. I know I am.'

Jemma shook her head. Her stomach still churned, and the foul smell lingered in her nostrils. 'I couldn't eat a thing.'

As Gertrude drove herself back to Burns Books, at a much more sedate pace, Jemma noticed Lennox and Luke conferring quietly. Lennox turned to her. 'Luke and I shall cover tomorrow.'

Luke was sitting with an arm slung around Maddy, who didn't seem to mind. 'I'll do the morning shift,' Lennox continued, 'and Luke can do the afternoon. While that's going on, we'll contact Guild members in London and see who is able to help.'

'Luke doesn't have to cover,' said Jemma. 'I can go in the afternoon.'

'I'm sure you could,' said Lennox, 'but you should rest. Just run your shop tomorrow and we'll take care of things. Don't worry, we'll keep you informed.'

So after forcing down a ham sandwich at Burns Books, Jemma had returned to the Friendly Bookshop, escorted by Luke, inspected every corner and found nothing suspicious, and fallen into bed in her clothes. *I should check on the cats*, she thought, as she slid into sleep.

***

The door of the Friendly Bookshop opened and Lennox walked in. 'You seem brighter,' he said, with a forced jollity. 'Nothing suspicious to report, and Luke has taken over the watch.'

'Oh. Good.' She half-expected him to leave, but he stood there, fidgeting with a glove.

'Um, I managed to speak with Raphael.'

'Oh?' Jemma had considered contacting Raphael that morning, but her head was still too jumbled to conduct a sensible conversation. She had woken to a blaring alarm at a quarter to nine, stumbled to the bathroom to wash her face and brush her teeth, and gone downstairs to open the bookshop, refilling the cats' bowls on the way. 'What did he say? Did you tell him about last night?'

'I did, yes,' said Lennox. 'He was surprised, to say the least. He wants to speak to you when you're ready.' He paused, and studied the shelves next to him. 'But he will stay in Italy for now.'

'I see.' Jemma looked at Lennox, wondering whether she should feel something.

'So I'm still running things.' His mouth quirked up at one corner. 'It isn't quite what I expected when I agreed to take this on. I have various other commitments, as you know.'

'Has cover been arranged for the British Library tomorrow? If not, I can do it. Maddy can mind the shop.'

'But what if there's a knowledge emergency somewhere else? Besides, I need you to manage Burns Books. I have a book chapter to write for an old colleague of mine, and it's already a week overdue.' He flashed a winning smile at her, but it had no effect.

'What would have happened if we hadn't gone to the library yesterday evening?' Jemma asked. 'Would it still be there this morning?' She stared at him, tall and authoritative in his pinstriped suit and overcoat. 'That's what we should be doing. I'm sorry, but I don't care about your book chapter or your other commitments. We have to stop Drusilla.'

'It's not that I disagree with you,' said Lennox, 'but I'm sure you've put a stop to any messing around for now. I need you to function as my Assistant Keeper and shop manager. We'll work on a plan while we conduct our usual business—'

'Then I resign.' Jemma hadn't known she was going to say the words until they hung in the air between them. 'This has to be the priority, and if it isn't yours, it's mine. Maddy and I can run the Friendly Bookshop, and I can assist in knowledge emergencies, but I can't chair committees and do paperwork and mind your shop with this going on.' She held his gaze. 'And I can't cover your absences.'

Lennox looked at his feet, then at her, and where she had expected anger there was neutrality. She wasn't sure if that was worse. 'In that case, I accept your resignation. I hope you will continue to fulfil at least some of your duties while I recruit a replacement.'

'Of course,' she said, but he was already turning to leave.

What have I done? On impulse, Jemma went into the stockroom and approached the shelf where she had placed a powerful book of recipes. *Will it let me go near? I can't say that I'm an Assistant Keeper any more. What am I?*

She took another step. *I'm still me. I'm Jemma, and I run this bookshop. This is my stockroom, and I'm in charge. And I defeated Drusilla yesterday evening. If that isn't enough, I don't know what is.*

Jemma took one more step and laid her hand on the spine of the book. A slight tingle made her draw back; then she realised she had used her sore right hand. When she touched the book with her left hand, it felt normal. She drew the book out, checked its pages, and sighed with relief. *I still have my powers. They haven't left me.*

'Jemma?' It was Maddy's voice. She came out of the stockroom and found herself face to face with Maddy, who wore a distinctly worried expression. 'I wondered where you were.'

'I'm fine,' said Jemma. 'I was checking something.'

'Oh, that's all right then.' Maddy smiled. 'It's just that after yesterday—'

'I have some news, Maddy. I've handed in my resignation as Assistant Keeper. I'll still work here, but I need to give most of my time to stopping Drusilla.' Jemma shrugged. 'Someone has to.'

Maddy looked less shocked than Jemma had expected, though the smile had left her face. 'And I'll help you. I'll do everything I can.'

They both jumped as Jemma's phone rang. But it wasn't her new phone. It was the old one.

Jemma took it from her pocket. The display said *Carl*. *Lennox has unblocked my phone.* 'It's Carl. Do you mind if I…?'

'Of course not,' said Maddy. 'Why don't you go upstairs?'

'Thanks.' Jemma pressed *Answer*. 'Hello?'

'I wasn't sure if you'd answer,' said Carl. 'We keep missing each other.'

'We do, don't we.' Jemma climbed the stairs and unlocked the door of her flat.

'Can you talk?' Carl sounded almost apologetic. 'I wasn't sure if you'd be on your lunch.'

'Yes, I'm on my lunch,' said Jemma, putting down her keys and closing the door. 'How's the play?' She glanced around for Folio and Luna. *Odd that they're not here already, meowing for food.*

'The play's fine, but that isn't why I was ringing. The theatre's closed next Wednesday for electrical work, so we've all got a day and a night off. Can I come and see you? I know it's too late for Valentine's Day...'

'Valentine's Day?'

'Yes, you know, tomorrow.'

Squeak. It had come from upstairs.

'Hang on a minute,' said Jemma. 'Luna's shut in the bathroom.'

Squeak. The sound was very high-pitched.

'I'm coming,' said Jemma, climbing the stairs. 'What are you squeaking for? I can see the door's open—'

She stopped dead in the doorway.

Luna was reclining on a towel which lay on the bathroom floor. Attached to her, and busy feeding, were four kittens: a black one, a ginger one, a tortoiseshell one, and a tuxedo one.

The tuxedo kitten appeared to be wearing black cycling shorts. He lost his grip, squeaked, and latched back on. Folio sat watching nearby, amber-eyed, sleek, and every inch the proud father.

'Jemma, are you still there?'

'Yes, I'm still here.' Jemma crouched beside Luna and gently stroked her head. Luna rumbled a purr. 'Clever girl,' she whispered.

'Jemma, who are you talking to? I thought you were seeing to Luna.'

'I am,' said Jemma. 'And yes, please come and see me.'

Folio sauntered over and she tickled him under the chin. 'I've got so much to tell you.'

Acknowledgements

My first thanks go to my wonderful and very speedy beta readers – Carol Bissett, Ruth Cunliffe, Paula Harmon, and Stephen Lenhardt – and my excellent proofreader, John Croall. Any errors that remain are mine only.

In the same vein as the London Library in the previous book in the series, the Maughan Library and Charing Cross Library, as they appear in this book, are hopefully fairly similar in appearance and layout to the real thing, but the staff are entirely fictional.

As ever, my final thanks are for you, the reader. I hope you've enjoyed the book, and I promise that book 6 will be my next project! If you have enjoyed this book, a short review or a rating on Amazon or Goodreads would be very much appreciated. Ratings and reviews, however short, help readers to discover books.

FONT AND IMAGE CREDITS

Cover and heading fonts: Alyssum Blossom and Alyssum Blossom Sans by Bombastype.

Cats: Cat silhouette premium vector by freepik: https://www.freepik.com/premium-vector/cat-silhouette_718088.htm

Book buildings: Books engraving illustration by tartila: https://www.freepik.com/premium-vector/books-engraving-vintage-open-book-engrave-sketch-drawn-hand-drawing-student-reading-textbook-illustration_7394262.htm

Book bridge: Vintage book elements collection with different books Free Vector by macrovector: https://www.freepik.com/free-vector/vintage-book-elements-collection-with-different-books_9397979.htm

Stars: Night free icon by flaticon at freepik.com: https://www.freepik.com/free-icon/night_914336.htm

Cover created using GIMP image editor: https://www.gimp.org

About the Author

Liz Hedgecock grew up in London, England, did an English degree, and then took forever to start writing. After several years working in the National Health Service, some short stories crept into the world. A few even won prizes. Then the stories started to grow longer…

Now Liz travels between the nineteenth and twenty-first centuries, murdering people. To be fair, she does usually clean up after herself.

Liz's reimaginings of Sherlock Holmes, her Pippa Parker cozy mystery series, the Caster & Fleet Victorian mystery series (written with Paula Harmon), the Magical Bookshop series, and the Maisie Frobisher Mysteries are available in ebook and paperback.

Liz lives in Cheshire with her husband and two sons, and when she's not writing or child-wrangling you can usually find her reading, messing about on Twitter, or cooing over stuff in museums and art galleries. That's her story, anyway, and she's sticking to it.

Website/blog: http://lizhedgecock.wordpress.com
Facebook: http://www.facebook.com/lizhedgecockwrites
Twitter: http://twitter.com/lizhedgecock
Goodreads: https://www.goodreads.com/lizhedgecock
Amazon author page: http://author.to/LizH

Books by Liz Hedgecock

Short stories
The Secret Notebook of Sherlock Holmes
Bitesize
The Adventure of the Scarlet Rosebud
The Case of the Peculiar Pantomime (a Caster & Fleet short mystery)
Christmas Presence

Halloween Sherlock series (novelettes)
The Case of the Snow-White Lady
Sherlock Holmes and the Deathly Fog
The Case of the Curious Cabinet

Sherlock & Jack series (novellas)
A Jar Of Thursday
Something Blue
A Phoenix Rises

Mrs Hudson & Sherlock Holmes series (novels)
A House Of Mirrors
In Sherlock's Shadow
A Spider's Web

Pippa Parker Mysteries (novels)
Murder At The Playgroup
Murder In The Choir
A Fete Worse Than Death

Murder in the Meadow
The QWERTY Murders
Past Tense

Caster & Fleet Mysteries (with Paula Harmon)
The Case of the Black Tulips
The Case of the Runaway Client
The Case of the Deceased Clerk
The Case of the Masquerade Mob
The Case of the Fateful Legacy
The Case of the Crystal Kisses

Maisie Frobisher Mysteries (novels)
All At Sea
Off The Map
Gone To Ground
In Plain Sight

The Magical Bookshop (novels)
Every Trick in the Book
Brought to Book
Double Booked
By the Book
Black Books

For children (with Zoe Harmon)
A Christmas Carrot

Printed in Dunstable, United Kingdom